Just in time for June...
Janet Dailey's <u>The Hostage Bride</u>

It's been said that Janet Dailey "wrote the book"
on romance. And Silhouette Books is thrilled to
announce that Janet Dailey, America's best-loved
romance author, will now be writing for Silhouette
Romances, starting with *The Hostage Bride* in
June.

You may have enjoyed one of Janet's recent
novels: *Touch the Wind*, *The Rogue* or *Ride the
Thunder*. All three made *The New York Times*
best-seller list— and together sold well over three
million copies! Her latest book, *Night Way*, is
currently on the best-seller list, and is another
million-seller.

More than eighty million people have already
fallen in love with Janet Dailey. Her books have
been translated into seventeen languages and are
now sold in *ninety* different countries around the
world.

We're sure that you too, will fall in love with
Janet Dailey's romance novels. Be sure to watch
for *The Hostage Bride* this June.

Dear Reader:

Silhouette Romances is an exciting new publishing venture. We will be presenting the very finest writers of contemporary romantic fiction as well as outstanding new talent in this field. It is our hope that our stories, our heroes and our heroines will give you, the reader, all you want from romantic fiction.

Also, *you* play an important part in our future plans for Silhouette Romances. We welcome any suggestions or comments on our books and I invite you to write to us at the address below.

So, enjoy this book and all the wonderful romances from Silhouette. They're for *you!*

Karen Solem
Editor-in-Chief
Silhouette Books
P.O. Box 769
New York, N.Y. 10019

TESS OLIVER
Double or Nothing

Silhouette Romance
Published by Silhouette Books New York
America's Publisher of Contemporary Romance

Other Silhouette Romances by Tess Oliver
Red, Red Rose

Quote from "November Surf" by Robinson Jeffers copyright
1932, © 1960 by Robinson Jeffers, is taken from *The Selected
Poetry of Robinson Jeffers,* copyright 1938, © 1966 by Donnan
Jeffers and Garth Jeffers. Used by permission of Random
House, Inc.

SILHOUETTE BOOKS, a Simon & Schuster Division of
GULF & WESTERN CORPORATION
1230 Avenue of the Americas, New York, N.Y. 10020

ISBN: 0-671-57078-1

First Silhouette printing May, 1981

10 9 8 7 6 5 4 3 2 1

America's Publisher of Contemporary Romance

Printed in the U.S.A.

For Marie and Frank—
good parents; good people; good company. . . .
with thanks and deepest love.

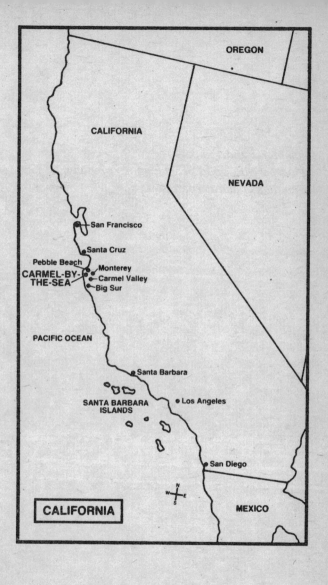

Chapter One

It was three o'clock on the Wednesday before Thanksgiving and the rush and bustle of the day had finally abated enough for Leigh Mallory to relax, lean back in her thronelike old oak captain's chair, and enjoy being the monarch of all she surveyed.

Leigh was too young to look regal, but the promise for later years was there. A discerning eye would have seen the potential in her proud posture and the classical bone structure of her face. Her natural good taste was reflected in the black-and-white houndstooth wool skirt she wore with a plainly cut French-cuffed silk blouse, and in the restraint of the small round silver earrings in her pierced earlobes.

Today her cloud of hair lay against her shoulders in drifts of luxuriant butterscotch and cream and her intelligent eyes were a warm, golden-flecked brown. But something about her suggested that someday her hair would be a dignified coronet of burnished gold and her eyes a warm and wise amber.

Leigh sighed now with the pleasantly virtuous feeling of a day's work well done and looked about her tiny domain with a smile on her generously wide mouth. Not that her kingdom would seem all that much to a more objective eye; but to Leigh the small one-room office a half-story beneath street level, with the hand-painted sign outside reading "MALLO-RY REALTY," was still a new and soul-satisfying triumph.

There was floor space for only two clients' chairs and two desks; one for herself, near the window that looked out onto Carmel-by-the-Sea's Ocean Avenue, and one for Leigh's younger sister, Dibbie, who now sat with the phone attached to her pink ear, her pretty pink bow of a mouth murmuring sweet foolishness to her latest boyfriend. On the walls of the small room were photographs of listings for sale, running the gamut of Carmel's exhilarating mix of architectural individualism. There were New England saltboxes, Mediterranean villas wrought small, English cottages with imported thatched roofs, charming Hansel-and-Gretel cabins tucked away in the forested hills, and elegant, ultramodern redwood houses with their soaring three-story glass walls fronting the magnificent blue Carmel Bay.

Dibbie had just exploded a small good-bye kiss into the phone when a pair of well-tailored male legs stopped in front of the office, their owner presumably scrutinizing the listings posted in the display case on the street.

"Oh, bother!" Dibbie sighed. "I hope he doesn't come in. I'm meeting the group at McFly's, and I want to go home first and change."

Leigh gave her sister a mock frown. "You'll never get ahead with an attitude like that, little sister."

"I don't want to get ahead," Dibbie smiled impishly. "I want to get a man. You're the real estate mogul in the family, not me."

With one eye on the man's legs, which seemed to be growing out of the window planter full of purple fuchsia, Leigh retorted, "I am not now, nor do I ever wish to be, a 'real estate mogul.' I want the same thing you do; I'm just in no hurry."

"Whoo! No hurry! That's the understatement of the century. Gran says you're too picky, and I agree. You've turned more men away than tourists in July."

Leigh laughed and shook her head in fond chagrin. "I know full well what Gran says. Haven't I heard it every day of my life since I was eighteen? But I'm *not* picky. It's just a case of once burned, twice shy."

"Oh, for heaven's sake, are you still beating that old dead horse? Who *hasn't* had a botched love affair by your age?" Then, with a teasing smile, Dibbie asked, "How old are you now? Forty-four?"

Leigh responded only with a disgusted look.

Dibbie snapped her fingers. "Now I remember. Gran says you're twenty-four going on forty-four. She says you were born with an old head."

Leigh laughed and said, "Gran has more opinions

in one week than most people could manage in a lifetime."

The tinkle of the doorbell alerted the sisters to the fact that the man, momentarily forgotten, was entering the office. Leigh watched as first his gray-pinstripe-trousered legs, then his well-tailored torso descended the wooden stairs, followed by a pair of broad shoulders, and finally, ducking to avoid the low lintel, his head of thick, wavy, sunlit black hair.

At the first sight of his face, Leigh felt as though a silent explosion had taken place somewhere behind her eyes. The small room seemed to flare into golden light, then darken to normalcy, leaving her feeling slightly queasy. As the man's deep blue gaze rested first on Dibbie's masses of yellow ringlets and her round, sweetly open face, Leigh stared at him. She saw, with quite astounding and unnecessary clarity, the firm line of his jaw, the delicate curve of his upper lip and the fullness of the lower, the pure slant of his elegant nose, and most disconcertingly of all, every intricate whorl of his left ear.

After bare seconds that had seemed like an aeon to Leigh, he favored Dibbie with a courteous smile, but turned to Leigh and spoke. "Good afternoon. My name is Dow Madigan, from New York City." At first, the baritone timbre of his voice sent a warm shudder up Leigh's spine, but then he went on to say, "I'm interested in acquiring property in your little storybook village," and as his words and their condescending tone penetrated her awareness, Leigh felt herself grow cool and stiff. Then, finally: "I wonder if I might speak to your broker," he demanded, more than asked.

Leigh involuntarily glanced at Dibbie, who, out of the stranger's range of vision, stuck her small nose into the air and pinched her mouth together in a mockery of his haughty pomposity. Suppressing a smile, Leigh stood up and offered the man her hand. "How do you do, Mr. Madigan. I'm Leigh Mallory, and this is my sister, Deborah. If you'll tell me a little about your requirements, I'll do my best to help you."

Nodding briefly to them both, the man smiled in lazy amusement. "I'm sure you would, my dear, but I prefer to speak to your broker."

With what she hoped was equanimity, Leigh answered, "I am the broker, Mr. Madigan."

The man looked startled; then with a narrow smile he raised his eyes to the ceiling and murmured, "Only in California."

Leigh responded coolly, "I beg your pardon?"

"Why, you're a mere child."

Leigh's usually warm golden-brown eyes frosted over. "Didn't you know that mere children are allowed to be licensed real estate brokers in California?"

Dryly he replied, "I don't doubt it, since the whole state seems to be run by children."

Leigh came from behind her desk and walked stiffly to the office door, as if seeing him out. "Perhaps you'll be more satisfied with another broker, Mr. Madigan. If you like, I can suggest several grown-up men who might suit your needs better."

He moved not an inch as he drawled suggestively,

"I sincerely doubt that, Miss—is it?—*Miss* Mallory?"

"Indeed it is," Dibbie suddenly spoke from behind her desk. The other two people in the tiny room turned as one to stare at her, as if they'd both forgotten her presence. With a nonchalance that didn't fool Leigh for one minute, Dibbie gathered up her jacket and handbag and sauntered to the door. "I'll just run along now, Leigh. I'm sure you can manage without me." Pausing at the door, she said to the tall man, "I do hope you'll find what you're looking for, Mr. Madigan. But you're bound to. If Carmel doesn't have it, it doesn't exist." And with an airy smile she waved herself out of the office.

Dow Madigan stood looking after Dibbie with a quizzical expression on his patrician face, then turned briskly to Leigh and returned to business as if nothing untoward had taken place. "I'd like to see one of those houses outside, if I may. The one above the beach that has four bedrooms."

That would be Minnie Wanamaker's house, Leigh thought. She glanced at her wristwatch and saw that it was nearly three-thirty. Minnie's nightly séance began promptly at six o'clock, and because she felt that the disturbing vibrations caused by strangers in the house took exactly two hours to dissipate, she refused to allow the house to be shown after four o'clock. Leigh would have freely explained this to any Carmelite client, but to this judgmental easterner she said only, "I'm so sorry, but that seller prefers the house to be shown only during the morning or early afternoon. If you like, I'll make an appointment for Friday morning."

With ill-concealed annoyance Dow Madigan said, "What's wrong with tomorrow?"

"Why, tomorrow is Thanksgiving," Leigh said, surprised. "It's not customary, on holidays . . . but I suppose I could call her."

The man frowned and turned his face away from her. "No, it just slipped my mind. Friday will be fine."

A surge of sympathy for him surprised Leigh. Imagine how alone one must be to forget Thanksgiving! But immediately she shrugged her sympathy away. From the way this man comported himself, anything smacking of pity would be anathema to him anyway.

Suddenly he swung his head toward her, quite like a frustrated caged lion, and said irritably, "Is there anywhere in this candy box of a town to get a drink?"

Taken aback by the ferocity of his tone, Leigh scoured her mind for a place to direct him that he wouldn't sneer at. But then she asked herself why she should care what this rude stranger thought anyway. Taking a leaf from Dibbie's book, she said pleasantly, "Obviously you haven't been in Carmel even an hour, Mr. Madigan, or you wouldn't ask that question. On the other hand, after you've been here a few days, you won't need alcohol to knit up the raveled sleeve of your care."

With a snort he said, "I'll look forward to that, Miss Shakespeare, but in the meantime, let's go have a drink." He took hold of her elbow and moved toward the door.

Leigh momentarily balked, more at his high-handedness than any real unwillingness to have a drink with him. On the contrary, his very outrageousness intrigued her. She felt . . . challenged, perhaps. There was a satisfying sharpness to him that most of the men she knew lacked. Besides, accompanying clients to bars and restaurants was an important part of her job.

When Leigh had justified her puzzling desire to remain in this imperious man's company, by designating him just one more client to be indulged and cosseted, she took her black wool blazer from the pine hook by the door and locked up the office for the night.

As Leigh walked down Ocean Avenue with the tall, silent man beside her, she thought: Surely he'll at least appreciate this divine weather. Nearly every day this month the beautiful little village had basked in clear, dry days bathed in that special cool-warm sunshine found only in close proximity to the Pacific Ocean. It was during the hectic summer months, when tourists glutted the streets and shops of Carmel, that the fog paid its visit daily. This delightful boon, that the finest weather of the year was reserved for Carmelites alone, did much to soften the ironic sting for many of the locals, that a town developed by artists and writers and musicians in search of privacy had evolved into a town completely dependent on tourist traffic for its economic survival.

The patio of the General Store-Forge in the Forest was sprinkled with locals sitting at tables under red-white-and-blue Cinzano umbrellas, chatting and drinking in the surprisingly strong November sun. Those who'd found no place in the sun sat huddled near either of the two large brick fireplaces, warming their thin California blood.

When their drinks had been served, Dow Madigan looked pointedly around him and said, "From what you said earlier, all these people must be as new to Carmel as I am."

Embarrassed at his reference to her own recent pomposity, Leigh smiled wryly. "Maybe I did exaggerate just a bit."

Dow Madigan returned her smile, and at this first break in the stiff formality of his expression, Leigh felt most of the tension between them evaporate in even less time than Minnie's vibrations.

By the time Leigh's prospective client was halfway through his second martini, he sat more loosely in the steel-mesh patio chair, his arm resting on the varnished pine table, and his expensively clad legs were stretched out to their full length on the well-worn brick floor.

With a deftness developed over the past three years, Leigh drew him out to tell her some of what she'd need to know to serve him well in his search for property. She learned that he'd driven across the country, arriving in Carmel just this afternoon after registering at the Highlands Inn a few miles south of the village. His company was opening a branch in the San Francisco area and he wanted a weekend beach house either in the Carmel area or in Santa Cruz.

"Most probably here," he said. "I understand I

15

can expect a faster appreciation rate here, also higher and more stable property values than in Santa Cruz."

"On the other hand," Leigh pointed out fairly, "Santa Cruz is much nearer to the city than Carmel is. You'd have nearly a two-hour drive from here, perhaps longer on weekends."

He waved a long-fingered, graceful hand in the air. "The difference in time will be negligible. I have a small plane."

"I see," Leigh said casually. But even though she moved, for the most part, in the world of the very rich, she was not of that world and she often thought she'd never learn to take their great wealth for granted as they themselves did.

Dow Madigan said nothing about his personal life, but because he asked her about Carmel's school system and specified that he wanted a large house, at least four bedrooms, within an easy walk to the beach, Leigh assumed that there were a wife and family in the east. But in that case, she wondered, why had he absented himself from them during such a family-oriented holiday as Thanksgiving?

She was just about to ask him point-blank if he was married—after all, it was a basic question for a broker to ask a client—when he hailed the waitress for the check.

"Please, allow me to take care of that," Leigh said, giving the girl an eye signal.

With a sarcastic smile he replied, "Of course. You're such a pretty girl, I quite forgot that you're a broker and I'm a deductible item."

Ignoring his insincere compliment, Leigh fixed

him with a level gaze. "If you like, but I'd thought of it more as a gesture to make you feel welcome in Carmel."

To his credit, Dow Madigan had the grace to look a bit embarrassed as they walked silently down the beaten-earth sidewalk on their way to Leigh's office. It was near five o'clock now and the streets were sparsely populated. What few tourists there were this time of year were probably resting up before dinner in the town's many inns and hotels, after a day's glorious shopping. The locals were closing up shop to return to their families at home. The air had a chill to it now and the light had dimmed enough that Leigh asked Mr. Madigan to watch his step.

"Until you're familiar with our unpaved side streets, it's easy to stumble over the tree roots that push through the ground."

"That's very sloppy municipal maintenance, isn't it?" he said, reverting to his previous superior tone.

Leigh shrugged. "Trees are sacred in Carmel. If a tree gets in the way of a house, or a person, or a street, it's never the tree that has to move. You'll see trees in the middle of streets and sidewalks and poking through holes in fences all over town."

"They could at least put up streetlights, then," he grumbled.

In response to his pettish complaint, Leigh said crisply, "They have streetlights in Santa Cruz, I believe. I'm sure you'd prefer that to carrying a flashlight with you at night, as we do here."

Leigh no longer cared a pin if she drove off an affluent client. Life was too short to spend time with an eastern fault-finder like Mr. Dow Madigan. When they reached Leigh's office, she waited for him to confirm their business appointment for Friday. If he didn't, she was more than willing to let this badly begun business relationship die a natural death.

Dow Madigan referred to Friday in no way; instead he leaned insouciantly against the Monterey cypress outside Leigh's office. "I understand Carmel has no mortuary or cemetery," he said with a hint of amused scorn in his tone.

"That's correct," Leigh replied shortly.

"Perhaps that's why so many old movie stars live here, to perpetuate the Hollywood delusion of immortal youth. Where there's no cemetery, perhaps there's no death," he said ironically.

Exasperated beyond all civility, Leigh let her dislike for this man color her voice as she said, "People live here, Mr. Madigan, *real people*. We have death and sickness and misery here, just like anywhere else. But this is a *very small village*. The village proper is less than a mile square, the native population is not quite five thousand people. There are many things we don't have here, as you've pointed out. We don't have paving on our side streets, nor streetlights except in the main shopping area, we have no mortuary, and no cemetery. We also have no live entertainment, not even jukeboxes, in our bars and restaurants, and no neon signs, because we treasure the peace and quiet and beauty of our natural environment. If you ever visit our city beach, I defy you to find so much as a discarded gum wrapper on it!"

Dow Madigan murmured something and reached out to touch Leigh's arm, and she wrenched away from his touch. Riding high on a wave of righteousness, she plunged on.

"We also have no house numbers and no home mail delivery because it's a Carmel tradition to protect the privacy of all. And finally, we have no jail here, Mr. Madigan, and on the rare occasion when a crime's committed, we use Monterey's jail. I can't imagine why you'd even consider buying property in a place you find so laughable. Maybe you'd better just stay in New York City where they have no lack of cemeteries or jails or people to put in them, either!"

Trembling with emotion, Leigh marched away from him toward her car, parked around the corner. From behind her she felt his strong grasp on her upper arm seconds before he whirled her around to face him.

There was absolutely no expression on his face from which Leigh could gauge what effect her outburst had had on him. He said with perfect aplomb, "There's just one—no, three more things I'd like to ask you, if you can spare a moment more."

Leigh looked down pointedly at his hand on her arm, and when he loosed her, she said begrudgingly, "What?"

"First, do you know a good lawyer?"

"Mr. Madigan, surely your company retains a law firm that could give you referrals. I'd rather not advise you on a matter like that."

"*Miss Mallory*"—he stressed the formality, subtly mocking Leigh's loftiness—"I'd like the suggestion of a local person who's *au courant* with the area's professionals, a person like yourself. Please. Even if I don't deserve your help."

Leigh sighed heavily, feeling much put upon by the tardiness of his oblique apology and his appeal to her good nature. "Oh, all right," she said ungraciously. "Sam Nelson is a very gifted lawyer. You'll find him in the phone book. We *do* have Yellow Pages in this barbaric wilderness, you'll be surprised to learn."

With a small smile, Dow Madigan took a black leather notebook about the size of a passport case from the inner pocket of his gray pinstripe suit coat and wrote down Sam's name. Then with his gold pen poised above the notebook, he asked, "And the name of several good women's clothing shops?"

Against her will, Leigh squirreled away this nut of information about his personal life and gave him the names of several shops, including that of her friend Pamela, who carried most of the California *haute couture* designers. No doubt nothing but the best would be good enough for Mrs. Madigan, Leigh thought meanly.

"And now, one last question, Miss Mallory. Do you happen to know if Persia Parnell, the old silent-film star, is still among the lotus-eaters here in never-never-land?"

Leigh was grateful that it was now too dark for him to see her start, or the shutters of caution film her eyes. "Yes, she is. Why do you ask?"

"Oh, no particular reason, except that my grandfather seems to have known her quite well at one time, and he spoke of her so often I thought it would be amusing to pay her a call. I don't suppose there's a map to the stars' homes, *à la* Hollywood?" he asked with a scornful smirk.

"Certainly not," Leigh replied shortly. "And, now if you'll excuse me, Mr. Madigan . . ."

"One more thing," he called after her retreating back. "Can you recommend a good restaurant?"

Without turning, Leigh called over her shoulder, "There are no bad restaurants in Carmel, Mr. Madigan."

"Will I see you Friday, then?" he called more loudly.

"I'll see what I can do," Leigh called back as she rounded the corner; then in grim silence she recited to herself the classic rebuff: Don't call me, Mr. Madigan, I'll call you.

Chapter Two

Not even Charles Dickens himself, Leigh thought, could have imagined a more cheery, untroubled, and loving familial picture than she was so fortunate as to be a part of tonight, as every night. The sitting room that she'd known since childhood, decorated in shades of cozy tans and rose, was warmed against the chill November night by the crackling fire in the huge stone fireplace at one end of the room. On the other end, the mahogany sideboard stood as it always had between the two high casement windows. In its exact center a pyramid of polished apples nestled in a gleaming brass bowl, flanked on one side by a vermeil bowl of walnuts and on the other by a silver tray holding a carafe of sherry and six silver liqueur cups. Hidden within the antique breakfront, the good stereo Leigh and Dibbie had bought Gran several Christmases ago played Handel's *Water*

Music, soothing enough to smooth the most frazzled of nerves, one would think.

Dibbie lounged deep in the soft indulgence of the old rose-patterned wing chair by the fireplace, dreamily filing her fingernails, her yellow curls turned to spun gold by the fire's glow.

In the middle of the room stood the large round table covered in green felt cloth. Kindly light from a ceiling-hung Tiffany lamp in pinks and reds haloed the heads of the five people sitting beneath it, all gathered there for a common purpose, as they had every Wednesday evening in living memory. In addition to Leigh, the four others were all residents of Illyria, Gran's beloved house, turned apartment house for the past twenty years. Gran, Burt Cosgreve, and the Channings—loved ones all. So why, Leigh asked herself, did she feel so strangely removed, as if she belonged somewhere else entirely?

"Leigh!" Gran's voice was impatient. "You've been woolgathering all evening. Are you going to see or fold?"

"What? Oh, I'm sorry, Gran," Leigh said distractedly. "I'll fold."

John Channing protested, "You're folding with four hearts up? At the very least, you've got a good bluffing hand there."

"Now, John," his wife, Annie, remonstrated, "you just play your own hand. Leigh knows what she's doing."

Gran muttered, "I'm not so sure of that," and deftly dealt the last down card to the remaining bettors.

As John Channing looked at his last card, the

hopeful look in his round blue eyes faded. "Nuts. I'm out."

"So near and yet so far, John?" Burt Cosgreve asked, tossing a blue chip into the pot. "Ten thousand," he said succinctly.

Annie Channing scrutinized her hand, then Burt's expressionless face. "I'll bet you're bluffing again, Burt."

"Only cost you ten to find out, Annie," he replied.

"Too rich for my blood," Annie said, sighing as she turned her cards neatly down in front of her.

Gran's beautiful brown almond-shaped eyes glowed with the excitement of competition as she said with relish, "I'll raise you ten thousand, Burt."

"Your loss is my gain, dear lady." He tossed another blue chip into the pot and spread out a pair of aces and three queens. "Can you beat a full house?"

"Oh, shoot!" Gran said, throwing in her hand. "I thought you were bluffing too!" Reaching a be-ringed, manicured hand across the table, she turned over Leigh's discarded hand. "Look here! Leigh threw in a flush!"

Leigh said defensively, "Burt's full house would have beat me anyway, Gran."

"That's not the point, child. You know you should always play a hand for all it's worth. You never know what's going to happen. Burt might *not* have had a full house, especially if you'd stayed in."

"Oh, Gran, what difference does it make!" Leigh cried with uncharacteristic impatience. "It's not even real money!"

The four older people exchanged shocked glances, then one by one murmured soothingly that it was late anyway, time for a break, Leigh worked so hard, she must be tired.

From the other end of the room came Dibbie's insinuating young voice. "Ask Leigh about the client who came in today, Gran."

Leaping on this diversion, the old people all fixed their gaze on Leigh as Gran said brightly, "Yes, darling, tell us about the new client."

Leigh pierced her sister with a chill look. "I don't know what Dib means, Gran. There's nothing to tell. He was just some man."

As one, the four gray heads turned for clarification to Dibbie, smiling catlike from the big wing chair. "'Some man' is right! Just about the best-looking man I've ever seen."

The heads swung back to Leigh, who sniffed, "He may have been good-looking, but he had the personality of Attila the Hun."

Dibbie protested, "Oh, come on, Leigh. A stand-in for Santa Claus, he wasn't. But he could've been worse."

"I suppose he could've been an ax murderer," Leigh agreed tartly. "You saw him at his *best*, Dib. I had to spend over an hour with him."

"Really? Tell us about it," Dibbie coaxed.

Annie Channing, her eyes bright with curiosity, said, "First tell us what he looked like, dear."

"Oh, for heaven's sake," Leigh said with exasperation. "He was tall. He had black hair and blue eyes. Nothing much."

In a disappointed tone, Annie murmured, "He doesn't sound especially good-looking. . . ."

"Oh, but he *was,*" Leigh quickly contradicted herself. "The fact is, he looked like an eighth-century Black Irish prince. And behaved like one, too."

The others in the room, not accustomed to flights of poetic fancy from their dear, sensible Leigh, again exchanged wary looks.

Gran said, "What was his name, dear?"

"Dow Madigan," Leigh replied shortly. "He said he was from New York City."

Because Leigh was looking down at her hands twisting in her lap, she didn't see the alert, quizzical look that came into Gran's expressive eyes.

Burt asked, "How do you mean, 'he behaved like an eighth-century prince,' Leigh? That's a very interesting remark."

Leigh sighed, wondering why the familiar interest Gran and the others took in her work should make her feel, tonight, as if she were a criminal undergoing the third degree.

"I just meant that he was arrogant and self-centered. Just a bigoted snob, really. Now, can we please change the subject?"

John Channing complained, "But you haven't told us anything yet!"

"What do you mean, 'bigoted'?" Burt persisted.

"Oh, you know what I mean, he was just the typical easterner with that typical supercilious attitude toward California. He called Carmel a candy-box town and 'your storybook village,' referred to the Hollywood 'delusion of immortal youth,' that kind of thing."

Now that she'd repeated Dow Madigan's slurs out loud, Leigh was puzzled that she'd reacted so strongly at the time. Californians were used to insults from easterners.

Burt shrugged. "That's nothing. East is East, and West is West, and never the twain shall meet—until they see what they're missing out here, that is."

The others all laughed and nodded in agreement. But perversely, Leigh resented their dismissal of what she herself just seconds before had seen as mere forgivable envy, which easterners often cloaked in scorn and petty carping. Her face flushing, Leigh repeated the one remark of Dow Madigan's that truly had upset her. "Also, he had the gall to ask if you were 'still among the lotus-eaters in never-never-land,' Gran. It seems his grandfather used to know you, and this . . . Dow person thought it might be 'amusing' to pay you a call."

"I knew it!" Gran cried triumphantly. "As soon as you told me his name, I *knew* it must be Dow's grandson." To the room at large she said, "Isn't that the most amazing coincidence? That Dow Madigan's grandson should run into my granddaughter? Why, I do believe Fate has had a hand in this."

Leigh's mouth dropped open in astonishment. Always beautiful, now Gran's thin, elegant face had taken on a joyful inner glow, her dark almond-shaped eyes shining with some precious secret memory.

The attention of everyone in the room abandoned

Leigh and fixed on—not Gran, not Jane Campbell from Detroit, not their easygoing landlady—but on the ultimate sex goddess of the twenties and thirties, the peer of Navarro and Valentino, the glittering star of stage and silver screen—Persia Parnell.

Leigh said weakly, "Then you did know his grandfather? I thought he was probably just another celebrity hound that you'd once sent a photo to, or an autograph. You know how they always exaggerate . . ." Leigh lapsed into thought, then added, "But he did say his grandfather spoke of you often."

A tender look came over Gran's face. "Did he say that, really?" She sighed pleasurably. "Darling Dow. I must admit, I've thought of him often enough, over the years."

Dibbie asked, "Then you *were* good friends, Gran?"

A charming pink flush stole over Gran's soft cheeks. "In a manner of speaking, yes, darling. We were very close at one time."

Dibbie and Leigh exchanged an amused and knowing smile. Among five marriages, Gran had managed to find room in her life for a good many "close friends" as well.

Annie Channing, with a rapt young smile on her mouth, said eagerly to Gran, "Wouldn't you like to meet the young man, Jane?"

As if coming out of a dream, Gran shivered slightly and smiled around the table. "But of course. We'll invite him to share Thanksgiving dinner with us tomorrow. Go along now, Leigh darling, and give him a call. Tell him Miss Parnell will be pleased to see him. Four o'clock, I think, don't you, Annie?"

"Gran!" Leigh cried in horror. "I can't call a perfect stranger and invite him to Thanksgiving dinner!"

Burt Cosgreve shook his finger at Leigh. "My dear girl, you're forgetting your history. Who better to invite than a stranger? That's one of the main purposes of Thanksgiving, after all."

Gran nodded in agreement, and added, "Besides, he's not a stranger to *me*—exactly," and again flushed pink.

Leigh felt desperate. She couldn't call that awful man—not after what he'd said to her and what she'd said to him. In a pleading tone she said, "Gran, I don't *like* him. *Please* don't ask me to call him. Can't you have him to tea Sunday or something? Why should he come here and ruin our holiday?"

John Channing had listened to this discussion with all the avidity of a child eavesdropping behind the newel post. "I can't wait to meet him. He must be really something if our Leigh dislikes him so much."

Leigh groaned and rolled her eyes as she saw the four old people and her treacherous sister all smirk knowingly, as if she were some silly hysteric who'd tipped her hand by protesting too much. With great dignity she rose from her chair. "If it will please you, of course I'll call him, Gran." And she walked on shaky legs toward the phone in the entry hall.

As luck would have it, he was in. Before she'd had a chance to prepare what to say, the inn's operator put her through to him.

"Madigan here," he said in that arresting baritone.

29

"Ummm, this is Leigh Mallory, we met earlier today?"

After a second's pause he said, "Yes?" and Leigh detected amusement, mild scorn, and triumph—all in that one syllable.

"I don't think I mentioned earlier that my sister and I live with my grandmother?" With irritation she realized she was asking him, not telling him. "And my sister . . . just happened to mention that a . . . newcomer to town had come into the office today. And my grandmother wondered if you'd like to join us for Thanksgiving dinner tomorrow?"

She heard him breathing into the silence, and a sudden clear picture of the exact color of his skin flashed before her mind's eye, crowding everything else out. It was not pale in that way eastern skin is often pale, from a lack of sun and an excess of anxiety, but ivory fair, like fresh, rich milk. To dispel the unwanted vision, Leigh plunged into words. "I'm sure you have other plans, but Gran just thought—"

"*No*," he interrupted with some force, then more smoothly went on. "I'd be most delighted to join you. And your sister and grandmother."

"Oh," Leigh replied weakly. "How nice. There'll be others here as well. In fact, Sam Nelson, that lawyer I mentioned? He'll be here. Well, fine then," Leigh said, anxious to disconnect from him.

"Perhaps you'd care to tell me where you live," he said in an amused tone.

She gave him the detailed directions necessary for strangers because of the absence of house numbers in Carmel, and Gran's phone number in case he got lost, a common occurrence to new visitors.

"The name of the house is Illyria, it's on a sign on the front fence. We'll see you around four, then."

"I'll look forward to it, and please tell your grandmother I'm very touched by this example of California hospitality."

Leigh examined this remark for possible irony or insult, and finding none, agreed to deliver the message and hung up.

Thanksgiving Day was dressed in crystal air and adorned with golden sunlight. Around ten in the morning all the residents of the house left their own apartments and tiny kitchenettes to meet for a convivial but sparse breakfast in Gran's large, sunny kitchen, which for today, like all holidays at Illyria, became the command center of the huge, rambling old house.

Because Leigh was the oldest of the younger members of this extended family of kith and kin, the responsibility for the actual mechanics of this harvesttime feast devolved to her, and it was she who parceled out chores and duties to her elders and to Dibbie.

Burt Cosgreve was in charge of the turkey—from purchase, through stuffing and basting, to carving. It was his position as de facto "man of the house" that qualified him for this most important job, as much as the fact that he was a retired food broker and presently a highly successful writer of cookbooks.

John and Annie Channing, retired musicians from

the Philadelphia Symphony Orchestra, in their mid-seventies and ten years Burt's senior, were in charge of preparing the mince and pumpkin pies and the brandied fruitcake for dessert.

Gran, notwithstanding her status as the owner of the house, or her professional renown as a famous movie star, or even her exalted position, at eighty years of age, as the eldest resident of the house, was relegated to the lowliest of KP duties. Never having had the time or inclination to achieve any culinary brilliance, she was set to peeling the white and sweet potatoes, the pearl onions, and to opening jars and bottles for the relish plate.

Dibbie's primary duty had been to do the marketing, and today, to set the table and arrange the centerpiece. Leigh's task, in addition to that of administration, was to clean up after dinner—with Dibbie's help, if that will-o'-the-wisp could be captured before she escaped with whatever current beau had joined them for the festivities.

Everything was proceeding smoothly by early afternoon, and Leigh went upstairs to her apartment to bathe and dress. She and Dibbie had the two suites in the house with no kitchens, since they took all their meals with Gran. The sisters' suites each consisted of a small bedroom and a very large sitting room with a view of the Pacific. They shared the bathroom that adjoined each suite.

The other two apartments each had their own bathroom, as small as the kitchenette, but as cunningly arranged for maximum use of space. Twenty years ago, when Gran had realized that her only asset, her beloved house, would have to become her livelihood as well, she'd spared no expense in the right areas. A retired architect, famous on the west coast for his brilliant use of space, and just coincidentally once a "close friend" of Gran's, had drawn the plans and acted as contractor for the remodeling.

Leigh and Dibbie had often remarked how lucky it was that the diverse personalities in the house had melded so congenially. The Channings had been here ten years, and Burt for twelve. Leigh and Dibbie had lived with Gran for ten years, since Leigh had entered high school and it was thought that the peripatetic life of the Army brat was no longer to the girls' advantage.

Soaking in bubbles up to her chin, Leigh thought now how much she wished her mother were here for today's holiday instead of in West Germany, where her stepfather was a base commander. She hoped that at least they'd come for Twelfth Night, since her mother had written that her stepfather, never one much for close family ties, wanted to spend Christmas at a ski resort in the Alps this year.

Leigh and Dibbie sometimes talked about what their lives might have been like if their own father, a handsome and charming rake, hadn't abandoned his wife of five years and his small children, to pursue the exciting and dangerous life of a Hollywood stunt man, which eventually killed him.

As Leigh dressed now, she resisted all generous thoughts of the stranger who was coming to dinner. It was true, she admitted to herself, what both Dibbie and Gran accused her of: she *was* very wary of romantic love. Everything she knew in her twenty-four years had served to convince her that love was but a snare and a delusion for a woman: Gran's five marriages; Gran's daughter—Leigh's own mother's rapturous but tragically short-lived marriage; and her own painful and humiliating baptism at eighteen when the young man she would have died for got cold feet a week before their wedding and left her to live on brown rice and bean sprouts in an Oregon commune.

In view of her negative opinions about love, Leigh preferred not to dwell on why she'd taken such particular care with her appearance today. Instead, she merely splashed her favorite spicy cologne behind her ears and on her wrists, and scrutinized herself in the full-length mirror attached to her closet door.

She'd chosen a lightweight wool dress in an autumn color somewhere between pumpkin and copper. It had an empire waist that set off her rounded bosom in a provocatively modest way, then fell gracefully over her hips to the currently stylish length. Around her throat she wore the amber necklace Gran had given her for her twenty-first birthday, three years before, and on her ears the gold dome earrings her mother had sent from Florence. Her shoes were simple brown pumps with a tortoiseshell pilgrim buckle on the instep. Giving her tawny hair one final flip, Leigh ran lightly down the broad stairway to join her family.

Chapter Three

When Leigh entered the sitting room she saw that everyone was there but Dow Madigan. She greeted Sam Nelson with a friendly social kiss, then left him to his conversation with Burt. Sam, a man in his mid-thirties, was a regular visitor to Illyria as one of Leigh's escorts. Divorced and the absentee father of three small children, Sam suited Leigh very well because his attitude toward emotional commitments was as cautious as her own.

Dibbie was in deep conversation with Ray Snelling, her latest boyfriend, a sweet but callow twenty-three-year-old medical student at the University of California at San Francisco. Because they seldom saw each other due to Ray's heavy class schedule and the distance between Carmel and the city, they conducted their romance mostly on the telephone. Leigh didn't intrude on them now, but took a seat near Gran.

The infallible sense of style that had so enhanced the film career of Persia Parnell had never waned, so that even at eighty years Jane Campbell effortlessly became the center of any assemblage by the mere force of her presence. She sat now in the high-backed wing chair by the fire, dressed in a simply cut mauve dinner dress adorned only by four strands of very good costume pearls. Her luminous white hair was done in her everyday fashion, winged back from her aristocratic face in an artfully arranged chignon.

"You look very beautiful, my dear," Gran said now to Leigh, reaching over to press her grand-daughter's hand. "And you're as good as you are beautiful. I thank God every day that my old age is blessed with you and Deborah."

Leigh opened her mouth to reply when the old-fashioned doorbell chimed through the room, and at just that instant Leigh was struck with a horrible thought. She'd forgotten, in yesterday's flustered state, to tell Dow Madigan that Gran was Persia Parnell!

Leigh jumped to her feet, her heart fluttering in panic. She had to reach him first—to tell him—before Gran realized he didn't know who she was, before some hideous embarrassment occurred! Then it further dawned on her that since he *didn't* know, he must have thought her story of Gran's hospitable invitation was merely a feeble excuse for *Leigh's* desire to further their acquaintance. Oh, how humiliating—and how untrue! But an invitation to

Thanksgiving dinner—out of the blue—from a complete stranger? What else *could* he think?

John Channing, with his childlike curiosity, had posted himself near the entry hall, and Leigh's heart sank as she saw him now, darting from the room to usher in the day's last guest—a most profoundly unwelcome guest.

However, in the next few seconds, as Dow Madigan entered the room and walked toward Gran to be introduced, whatever he may or may not have believed about Leigh's intentions before his arrival paled into insignificance.

Even before he reached Gran, Leigh saw that he'd instantly recognized her. The shock on his face was plain to see, for anyone looking for it, as Leigh was. But he recovered himself so quickly that Leigh was sure no one, especially Gran, noticed it. Affording Gran all the deference she was long used to and still enjoyed, Dow bowed low over her hand and murmured, "I'm honored, Miss Parnell."

As he straightened up he flicked a killing look at Leigh. Guiltily, Leigh stared mutely back at him, frozen by the icy glare of his dark blue eyes. Gran introduced him to the others in the room with an air that made him the honored guest, then sat him down across from herself, and in a flattering fashion, proceeded to monopolize him.

Leigh looked uncertainly around the room with an eye to escape, but Gran headed her off. "No need to leave, dear. Pull that ottoman over here and join us."

Leigh heard the order buried in the polite invitation and reluctantly obeyed. While these two power-ful personalities launched into the first stages of acquaintanceship, Leigh studied Dow Madigan from beneath downcast eyes. She had to agree with Dibbie that he was the most handsome man she'd ever met. Today he wore gray flannel trousers, a classic navy blazer, white shirt, and a gray-navy-and-maroon silk tie. His shoes were ankle-length boots of fine, supple leather. And if his clothes today were less severe than yesterday's, so too was the expres-sion on his face as he talked to Gran.

Suddenly noticing the shadowed expression on Gran's face as she listened to Dow, Leigh tuned in to the words being spoken by that arresting mouth, and heard, "It was while going through Grandfather's private effects that I came across the pictures of you. I think he must have had stills from nearly every one of your films. There were other references to you, as well . . ." Dow Madigan paused, as if to give Gran a chance to respond. When she didn't, he continued, "So, since I was coming west anyhow, I thought I'd take the liberty of calling on you, to tell you in person, in case you hadn't heard."

Gran's lips quivered and her eyes shone with unshed tears. "No, I hadn't heard. And if anything could make such sad news more bearable, hearing it directly from you has done so, Dow. Thank you very much for your thoughtfulness."

Leigh was disturbed to see the still-fresh grief on Dow's face, and she felt ashamed for not suspending judgment, as she'd certainly have done for anyone else, until she'd learned the reasons for his abrasive behavior yesterday.

Then, perhaps seeing how upset Gran was, Dow adroitly changed the direction of the conversation. Glancing at Leigh with a tight smile hidden from Gran, he said, "And wasn't it a pleasant coincidence that the first person I happened to speak to in Carmel turned out to be your granddaughter?"

Gran smiled happily. "Indeed it was. And I'm willing to bet that anything that begins so well must end well."

Dibbie walked up in time to hear Gran's remark, and said, laughing, "Gran, I do believe there's nothing you wouldn't bet on."

As they all moved at Dibbie's request to the dining room, Leigh gratefully took Sam Nelson's arm, assuming that Dibbie had seated them together at the table, as usual. And so she had. But Leigh soon saw that her sister had been up to her customary meddling, as well. Gran's card was at the head of the table, as always, and Burt's at the foot. Dow, as the honored guest, was at Gran's right, and Leigh had been squeezed between him and Sam Nelson, with Annie Channing on the end of the crowded side, next to Burt. John Channing sat on Gran's left, with Dibbie herself between John and her special guest, Ray Snelling. The three of them luxuriated in ample elbow room, while Leigh, on the crowded side of the table, could barely pick up a utensil without pressing into the arm of one of the men on either side of her.

Burt Cosgreve stood at the foot of the table, an avuncular smile on his still-handsome face, holding a bottle of wine in his hand. "We have not *one* honored visitor with us today"—he nodded and smiled at Dow—"but two. A liquor-broker friend of mine recently presented me with a case of Montrachet, the queen of all French white wines."

A little whir of awe and delight whispered around the table as Burt uncorked the wine and came around the table to pour Gran the first glass.

"That's a very impressive gift," Dow Madigan said genially. "I'd expected to be served California wine."

There was a sudden cautious silence in the room that held until Leigh, sorry now that she'd relented one iota toward this awful creature, said sharply, "Meaning that California wine is inferior to French wine, Mr. Madigan?"

With an expression of mock surprise, Dow turned to face Leigh and said innocently, "How paranoid you are, Miss Mallory. You remind me of a New Yorker."

Burt cleared his throat and raised his voice to simulate good cheer. "Now, Leigh, I'm sure Mr. Madigan meant no such thing. And as to that, my dear, any white wine in the *world* is inferior to Montrachet."

Fuming inwardly, Leigh smiled sweetly and replied, "No doubt you're right, Burt. However, if—by some peculiarity of taste—Mr. Madigan does in face *prefer* inferior wine, I think there's some New York State wine stuck away in the garage somewhere."

"Oh, I say!" John Channing remonstrated. "Let's not fuss over something as lovely as wine. Remember what Sir Walter Scott said: 'God in his goodness sent the grapes to cheer both great and small; little fools will drink too much and great fools none at all!'"

Amid laughter and cries of "Hear, hear!" Dow turned in his chair so only Leigh saw that the smile on his face hadn't reached his eyes. "Shall we bury the hatchet?" he asked lightly, then added with a menace so quiet that only she heard him, "For the time being."

The nervous laughter and anxious murmurs from the others at the table left Leigh no choice but to shrug and smile faintly in agreement. The two of them exchanged one last antagonistic glare as Gran suddenly pinged her knife vigorously against her wineglass, startling everyone into silence.

"I'd like to propose a toast, if I may." Gran glanced from Dow to Leigh with an enigmatic smile on her expressive face as she raised her glass and said, "May God bless all those who call these four walls home, and may He make these four walls home to all those here. Happy Thanksgiving, everyone!"

Gran's toast restored a festive feeling to the company that carried through from onion soup to mince pie. Even though Leigh kept her arms clamped close to her sides, Mr. Madigan seemed to take up an inordinate amount of space. Not only did his suited arm brush against hers throughout the meal—often on purpose to annoy her, she thought— but also she occasionally felt the touch of his knee against hers under the table as well. All this jostling caused by the intolerable scarcity of space at the table, plus the aroma of Dow's pungently spicy after-shave in her nostrils, served to make Leigh feel quite giddy and completely without appetite.

Dibbie, on the other hand, ate with her usual gusto. It was this love of food and her habit of spacing out her eating throughout the day—in "dibs and dabs," as she'd defended it as a child—that had given her the nickname she went by today.

Gran was in top form, regaling the company with the story of the time she'd attended a party at Pickfair, hosted by Charlie Chaplin, in honor of Lord Louie Mountbatten and his bride, Edwina, during the couple's honeymoon visit to America in 1922. "I was just twenty-two then, a year older than you, Deborah," Gran said reminiscently.

Dow Madigan asked Gran, "Had you met my grandfather at that time?"

"No, it must have been in 'twenty-nine or 'thirty that I met him, Dow. In the depths of the depression, it was. None of us had a dime during those years. But, do you know," she said thoughtfully, "I wouldn't trade that time for anything? Of course, it was easier for some of us. The fortunes some of us made, then lost, were more like play money than real money. Then too, we were young, we thought we had great expectations, and since we were all in the same boat, we helped each other. It didn't matter much that we lived from hand to mouth."

Sam Nelson interjected wryly, "I'm living from hand to mouth right now! When you can barely keep afloat from week to week, inflation and depression almost come to the same thing." The others laughed and ruefully agreed.

All but Dow Madigan, Leigh noticed. He listened quietly to the general conversation with an interested but noncommittal expression on his face. Leigh gave him good marks for not pretending that inflation touched the very wealthy in the same basic ways it touched more ordinary mortals. She'd met too many wealthy clients who bemoaned the cost of filling the gas tanks of their twenty-five-thousand-dollar cars or the skyrocketing cost of gold baubles to wear on their fingers and earlobes. Leigh held no brief against great wealth so long as those who possessed it also possessed a sense of responsibility for its proper use in society and an awareness that it didn't automatically make them superior to their less fortunate fellow beings.

Throughout dinner, every member of the company had been graced by Dow's attention and charm—everyone but Leigh, that is. However, Leigh noticed that most of all he'd seemed to court Gran; and that lady had opened like a rose under the sunshine of his attention. By the meal's end the two of them were as comfortable with each other as friends of many years.

This camaraderie carried over to the period after dinner, when brandy and liqueurs were served in the sitting room. Dow and Gran, his black, smoky head bent near her silvery white one, sat talking by the embers of the dying fire. John Channing coaxed Sam Nelson, Annie, and Leigh into a game of bridge. It has to be bridge because it was felt at Illyria that five was the minimum for a decent poker game, and Dibbie, as usual, flatly refused to play. She and Ray excused themselves, saying they were in dire need of a drive and some fresh air.

It was near nine o'clock when Leigh, usually as astute at bridge as she was at poker, went down doubled and redoubled, losing the rubber. She said to Sam, "I'm sorry, partner. I don't know what's wrong with me tonight."

"Never mind," Sam comforted her. "Just a run of bad luck." But Leigh had seen Sam look at her askance several times during the game when she'd made blockheaded plays only a beginner would make.

As he stood up, saying he had to go, Leigh felt a sudden panic, as if Sam's departure would leave her completely unprotected. "Oh, Sam, surely you don't have to leave so early!" she cried.

Her fervency surprised him. "I'm flattered, Leigh, but I really have to go. I'm getting up early tomorrow to drive into the city and bring the kids back for the weekend."

A few minutes later, Leigh had received Sam's brief good-night kiss and closed the door after him. She returned reluctantly to the sitting room and was relieved to see Dow Madigan saying his good-byes. From across the room Leigh watched him, a full head and shoulders taller than the older people circling him, looking up with smiles into his confident, darkly handsome face. Each and every one of them, Leigh could see, had succumbed to his insidious charm. As for Leigh, she would count the evening a success only when she saw the front door of Illyria close on his back; and for good, she devoutly hoped.

Gran saw Leigh standing at the doorway to the

room and called to her, "Come here, dear, Dow needs your assistance."

Now what? she thought warily as she walked slowly across the rose-and-tan Turkish carpet toward him, as if trudging across a vast and burning desert. As she neared him, his cool, oasis-blue eyes caught and held hers, and immediately she felt that unpleasant mixture of dread and fascination that so strangely afflicted her in his presence.

"I want you to take the flashlight and help Dow see his way to his car, Leigh darling," Gran said solicitously.

Leigh abruptly broke contact with the compelling blue eyes and looked at Gran aghast. In the past, Leigh had been the focus of Gran's matchmaking more times than she cared to remember, but never had it taken such a transparent and bizarre turn as this!

"Well," Gran said defensively, "Burt's coming down with a cold and John's knee is bothering him. He told me so before dinner. Didn't you, John?"

Listening with avid interest, John jerked into speech on hearing his name. "Oh! Yes. Yes, I did, Leigh. I clearly remember mentioning it to Jane."

Dow Madigan shrugged his wonderful shoulders and demurred, "I certainly don't want to cause any inconvenience. I've imposed on your hospitality quite enough. . . ."

Gran lifted her chin bravely and said with just the faintest hint of martyrdom, "Not at all, Dow. I, myself, will see you to your car, if you'll just let me get my wrap. I do so feel the chill at my age."

Leigh sighed gustily. "For heaven's sake, Gran! Of course I'll see Mr. Madigan to his car, if you like. I never said I wouldn't!"

All smiles and charm now that she'd won her point, Gran said her good-byes to Dow, taking his large hand between her own and making him promise her he'd come to see her again soon. "We'll have a nice long chat," she assured him.

John Channing's ailing knee didn't keep him from standing in the chilly draft of the open front door to watch Leigh and Dow walk all the way down the front path to the sidewalk before finally closing the door. Leigh cast the torch's pool of golden light before her and turned in the direction where Dow thought he'd left his car.

The night air seemed overly full of oxygen to Leigh. The chill made her blood race and her stomach flutter, as if she were somehow in danger, which was silly, of course. Still, when Dow suddenly reached over and took the flashlight from her and switched it off, a muffled cry escaped her dry mouth. "What . . . ?"

"Time to pay the piper," Dow said grimly, his voice very close in the crisp, taffeta blackness of the night.

"I'm sure I don't know what you're talking about," Leigh said, her voice tight with the effort to keep it from quavering. "Obviously you don't need my help to find your car. Please give me my flashlight so I can return to my house."

"No doubt you have more rewarding things to do than spend time with me, but—"

"*Much* more rewarding, Mr. Madigan," Leigh interrupted. "For instance, cleaning up the kitchen."

With that remark, Dow expostulated something Leigh was glad she hadn't heard clearly. Then he seized her by the shoulders as if to shake her. "Why didn't you tell me your grandmother was Persia Parnell?"

For a split second Leigh was speechless. She'd completely forgotten that there'd been an actual cause for his hateful attitude toward her all evening. She'd come to take his dislike to her as much for granted as her own for him. "I . . . well, I . . . just forgot," she said lamely.

Her eyes had adjusted to the dark enough for her to see his sarcastic smile. "No doubt a result of that mellow, laid-back California mentality."

Trying to jerk free of him, she said indignantly, "I don't have to listen to your provincial insults on my own property, Mr. Madigan."

Ignoring both her words and her attempts to free herself, Dow said heatedly, "You wanted me to make a fool of myself by not recognizing her, didn't you? You hoped I'd say something to hang myself—something critical of California, maybe, or Hollywood. You wanted me to commit a *faux pas* so serious I'd never be able to live it down, didn't you? Admit it!" he said, giving her one powerful shake.

Leigh grew alarmed. What was this madman raving about? Her face hot from fear and angry resentment, she pushed with all her strength against his superior bulk. "I don't know what you're talking about! But you flatter yourself if you think I'd expose my grandmother to hurt or embarrassment just to get at *you*. I *love* my grandmother," she retorted furiously. "I *said* it just slipped my mind! Now, let me go, you . . . you . . ." Leigh searched for an expletive strong enough to penetrate the barrier of his massive ego. "You . . . you . . . easterner!"

At her words his hands instantly loosened their grip, although he didn't let her go. Then there was a second of silence before, astoundingly, he threw back his head and a great peal of deep laughter rolled out into the listening night air. At this remarkable sound, Leigh's heart suddenly went as soft as butter in the sun. Still laughing, but more softly now, Dow pulled Leigh into the circle of his arms, and when she felt the rumbling vibrations of his amusement enter her own body from his chest, an odd but pleasant weakness overcame her legs so that she was forced to lean against him for support.

Dow buried his face into Leigh's tawny hair and sighed, as if exhausted by his recent merriment. "All right, California, I give up. You win this round. Although it's really beyond me," he murmured into her ear, "how it could've 'just slipped your mind' to tell me Miss Parnell was your grandmother when I'd expressly asked you about her."

Leigh stood trembling in the chill night, trapped so cozily in the warmth of Dow Madigan's embrace, and felt a strange lassitude come over her. Her whole body tingled like a numb limb suddenly wakened to life. How *had* she forgotten? she wondered vaguely. Last night, when she'd spoken to him on the phone and seen his face so clearly in her mind's eye, what emotion had filled her so full that all else was driven out? And it was happening again, she thought, gazing drowningly up into his deep blue eyes, her lids lowering dreamily as his face came closer and closer to hers. Her lips were helpless to resist his as they came to rest, warm and firm, on her mouth. His arms slid down to her waist, enfolding her tightly against his tall, hard body, making of the two of them a warm, throbbing entity, a world unto themselves.

Dow raised his lips from Leigh's briefly to whisper against her parted mouth, " 'Some lucky day each November great waves awake and are drawn like smoking mountains bright from the west . . .' " then broke off to kiss her hard on the lips, pressing her so close to him that she began to feel faint from a desire to be even closer to him . . . closer yet. . . .

Just then they heard a car engine close by, a door slam, and the quick, soft sound of Dibbie's small feet on the beaten-earth sidewalk, returning home from a tryst of her own.

"Oh! Hope I'm not interrupting anything important," she teased brightly as she swept past Dow and Leigh, each standing alone now and shivering slightly in the dampening, pine-drenched darkness.

Later that night, alone in her chaste bed, Leigh wondered how long she might have stood in Dow's embrace if Dibbie hadn't . . . saved her. She both dreaded and yearned to see Dow Madigan tomorrow, as they'd arranged. Turning restlessly in her bed, she wondered what to make of a man who sneered at California, at Carmel, yet, while kissing a woman, quoted to her from Robinson Jeffers, the poet who, above all others, understood and loved this land of rugged cliffs, wind-twisted trees, and beaches of pure white, virgin-clean sand.

Chapter Four

On Friday morning Leigh stared into her closet with uncharacteristic feelings of doubt and insecurity, searching for something to wear that would be appropriate to both her mood and her purpose: something attractive and lighthearted, and yet not frivolous. On the floor of the closet Leigh noticed the dark wine leather knee-high boots she'd bought on sale at I. Magnin's Memorial Day sale last spring. She always felt both chic and efficient when she wore those wonderful boots. So, using them as a point of reference, Leigh chose a plum-and-gray plaid wool suit with a cotton turtleneck top in a complementary rosy pink shade. Then, giving herself a final inspection in her full-length mirror, she decided the combination of her hair in loose waves and the romantically soft colors were too . . . yielding. Too feminine. So she twisted the errant tresses of hair into a soft bun and attached it to the back of her head. Yes, that was better. Now she looked like she was keeping a business appointment, not a romantic assignation.

However, five minutes after she picked up Dow Madigan that morning, Leigh saw that she might just as well have worn a thick yellow rubber mackinaw. From between nine and eleven o'clock she felt as though she were chauffeuring a thundercloud around town. Dow Madigan didn't care for the Petersen house because it had a detached garage. The Bentley house wouldn't do because it was an ugly color. The third, fourth, and fifth houses were, respectively, "too boring," "too bizarre," and "too bleak."

Dow delivered these judgments to Leigh in clipped, taciturn pronouncements, and with growing impatience, as if he were indeed a medieval prince to whom some scruffy merchant were offering one inferior piece of merchandise after another. Leigh was grateful, at least, that he waited until they were out of the sensitive owners' earshot before he damned each house.

After the fifth rejected property, Dow folded his tall body once more into Leigh's low-slung bronze Camaro and slammed the door. "If you recall, I did tell you I wanted to see that particular house on your display board. Or has that slipped your mind too?" he asked nastily.

Leigh snapped back, "And *I* told *you* that Miss Wanamaker asked us to come in the late morning.

You were the one who said we should look at some other properties first."

"Well, it's late morning now, so let's go there and get it over with," he said, staring stonily out the car window.

Leigh shoved the gearstick into low and muttered under her breath, "Your every wish is my command."

Dow glanced briefly at her and said with malicious sarcasm, "You're awfully cute when you're angry."

"Very funny." Leigh glared at him, then skidded away from the curb, heading west toward the ocean. The oppressive, tense silence that filled the car was very much at odds with the peaceful atmosphere of the green-canopied residential streets through which she drove.

Leigh had worked with uncooperative and unpleasant clients before, but this was ridiculous! After last night's unexpected and unwelcome intimacy, she'd expected a certain amount of embarrassment between them this morning, but she certainly hadn't bargained on such ferocious bad humor on Dow's part, nor such blatant dislike. What infuriated her was that he seemed to be blaming *her* for what had happened, and she silently called on heaven to witness that she'd been blameless! Why, she didn't even *like* the man, much less have any designs on him, if that's what he thought.

Leigh turned onto the street behind Gran's house, one street higher on the cliff that looked out over the city's white beach and the blue Pacific. She stopped the car in front of Minnie Wanamaker's large, imposing, boxy house of redwood and glass and shut off the engine. Dow got out of the car, and once again Leigh flinched as he slammed the Camaro's door. She joined him on Minnie's front path and waited beside him, feeling like some lackey in the lord's entourage, as Dow stood with his hands in his trouser pockets and surveyed the sight that lay below them.

He took a deep breath and exhaled slowly. "Now, this is more like it," he said with satisfaction.

Leigh too looked out and down, picking out well-known landmarks seen from a point of view just unfamiliar enough to give her a fresh insight into beauty too often taken for granted. There was her favorite cypress tree, at the edge of the beach near Scenic Road, balanced on an outbreak of rocks like a giant bonsai with its bone-white trunk blown horizontal by the prevailing winds, its deep green tufts of needles perched precariously on the tops of branches that stretched to escape the relentless sea winds, reaching toward the safe haven of the village of Carmel-by-the-Sea.

"Isn't that Illyria down there?" Dow asked, pointing at the brown-shingled cupola on Gran's roof, visible through the green cloud of trees that hovered over the houses below them.

"Yes, and over to the left, if you crane your neck a little, you can see Tor House," Leigh added helpfully—and then could have bitten off her tongue. A flush suffused her face as she cursed herself for bringing up Robinson Jeffers in any way whatsoever, even to point out one of Carmel's most prized possessions, the stone house he'd built on the cliff overlooking the sea. Now, because on impulse she'd behaved like some gushy tour director, this sour cynic, Dow Madigan, would surely think she was making some reference to last night when he'd so unaccountably quoted from Jeffers' poetry.

But Leigh needn't have worried. Dow, with an insulting blandness suggesting that he, for one, remembered no such intimate event ever taking place, said only, "I must make arrangements to visit Tor House while I'm here. I've heard so much about it." Then, turning to gaze at Minnie's dramatically beautiful house, he added casually, "Well, shall we look this shack over now?"

Minnie answered the door dressed in a ghastly flower-print cotton housedress, her mouth bristling with dozens of straight pins, looking for all the world like a North Dakota farmwife of the thirties. That is, except for her hennaed hair that she wore in Brillo fashion and the scarlet-taloned fingers with which she now deftly scooped away the pins in her mouth and cried, "Leigh, sweetheart! Come right in, I've been expecting you. I've just been doing a little sewing while I waited."

Leigh watched Dow's face as he looked askance, first at Minnie's short, chubby person and then at the lumpy little doll she held in her hand with its white muslin body and its gnarled head made from a withered apple. When the possible significance of the doll began to dawn on Dow, his eyes widened and a look of alarm stole over his handsome face, totally destroying his usual expression of correct eastern reserve. At the sight, Leigh's rankled heart was filled with delicious, if unworthy, glee.

As Minnie turned to lead them into the vast, airy reaches of the living room, Dow held Leigh back for a second and mouthed silently to her, "Is that a voodoo doll?"

Leigh smiled enigmatically and shrugged. Since he was so all-fired sure of everything, let him figure it out for himself, she thought smugly.

During the previous five property viewings Leigh had suffered through with Dow, he'd gone over each house with the speed and control of a roller coaster—up, down, zig, zag, and done. Minnie's house was no exception. Barely five minutes after they'd arrived, Leigh found herself standing once again in the living room, gentle sunlight pouring down on the three of them from the skylights in the fourteen-foot ceilings.

"Quite a house," Dow said casually, "not bad at all."

Leigh and Minnie raised an eyebrow at each other, but neither made any reply.

Dow said to Minnie, "I'd like to look at the layout of the upstairs again, if you don't mind."

"Be my guest," Minnie replied indifferently.

When Leigh moved to follow Dow, he drawled, "I remember the way," and she stopped in her tracks, flushing.

The two women watched him walk toward the open spiral staircase; one of them, at least, admiring the elegant carriage of his tall, slender body. Minnie crossed her arms over her ample bosom and thoughtfully stroked her dimpled chin with a red-tipped finger.

"I'd stay away from this one, Leigh," she said.

Leigh turned to stare at the older woman. "I have no intention of doing anything but!"

Minnie made a weary gesture. "I'm a busy person, sweets, please don't waste my time with that kind of talk. Any fool can see that you're gaga over him, it's written all over your face. But I'm telling you, he has a very nasty aura, sort of the color of an old bruise, all greenish-yellow."

Awed in spite of her basic rationality, Leigh breathed, "Really? What's wrong, do you think?"

Minnie shrugged. "Hard to tell exactly; deep unhappiness of some kind; he's heart-sore, that's for sure."

"His grandfather died recently; do you think that could be it?" Leigh asked hopefully.

"No," Minnie answered definitely. "Natural grief casts an entirely different-colored aura, not an ugly cloud like that." She sighed and shook her head. "It's a shame for such a good-looking man to be so miserable, isn't it? I wonder if he has a spiritual adviser," she mused.

Leigh hesitated, blushing for some ridiculous reason, then pressed on, forced to ask, "Can you tell if he's married? I mean, do you think it's a wife that's making him so unhappy?"

Minnie swung her gaze to Leigh, her lips pursed in disapproval. "You're not going to listen to me, are you? So typical of you people. That's the tragic paradox all us seers have to live with. As if it weren't bad enough to have to see these things in the first place, then you people ignore our warnings and we have to stand by helplessly and watch you plunge into perfectly avoidable messes." Minnie sighed in resignation. "But to answer your question, I can't tell if it's a wife or a lover, but I'm certain it's a woman. With a knockout like this one, Leigh, even you could guess that it's got to be a woman."

Leigh nodded sadly in agreement. Of course there had to be a woman, and a woman he felt very strongly about. Else she wouldn't have the power to cause Dow such pain. Here was just one more example of a truth Leigh had known for years now. The great Catch 22 of love was that in order to have it one had also to accept a vulnerability to pain. There was no way to have one without the other. Much better, Leigh thought, to forgo the dubious and fleeting pleasures of love and remain comfortable and heart-whole.

Mentally straightening her emotional spine, Leigh vowed to squelch her treacherously waffling emotions. Besides, even if she *were* drawn to this difficult, arrogant creature—which she certainly wasn't—he was already embroiled in a painful love relationship with another. Didn't he have a chartreuse aura to prove it?

By the time Dow returned to the living room, Leigh was quite proud of how thoroughly she'd shored up her defenses against the mysterious appeal he'd so briefly held for her. As he stood in the foyer saying good-bye to Minnie, Leigh noticed with complete disregard how the sunlight sparkled on his wavy black hair; she saw with total disinterest the fascinating shadows cast on the lean planes of his face; she heard with utter indifference the soft, deep, cultured tones of his voice.

After Minnie closed the heavy wooden door

behind them and they walked back to Leigh's car, she asked Dow, as she might have asked any visitor to Carmel, "We're only a few blocks from the beach. Would you like to see it up close?"

"I don't mind," Dow replied, slamming the door a bit more gently now.

As Leigh drove the short distance, she said nothing to break Dow's thoughtful silence. A real estate agent learns early on to say nothing about a property after a viewing until the client does, on the principle that no news is good news. And in Dow's case, the fact that he hadn't damned this house out of hand, like the others, was good news. Leigh drove down Thirteenth Street and onto the small jetty which gave pedestrian access to the beach as well as space for several cars to park and look out to the sea.

Leigh turned off the Camaro and then there was only the gentle ticking of the engine at rest to break the silence before them. It was nearly noon now and the sun, never directly overhead in California, was as high as it would climb that day. The blue sea was scattered with diamonds and the breakers foamed gently against the white sand. The serenity Leigh always felt here by the sea stole over her and eased her heart, so much in turmoil these last few days.

Leigh turned in the seat toward Dow, intending to share with him her pleasure, even her pride, in the calm grandeur of the view before them, this great union of the sea and sky, here at land's end. But Dow turned to meet her gaze and spoke first.

"It certainly is pretty. Looks just like a postcard."

Pretty! Postcard! Deep inside Leigh, some tender, budlike thing trembling on the verge of bloom wilted at Dow's crass words and folded in upon itself. In a cool, distant voice she asked him, "Shall I take you back to your car now?"

"Let me take you to lunch. No, I insist. Do you have a preference?" he asked lightly. "Or, since Carmel has no bad restaurants, shall we just blindfold ourselves and wander in somewhere willynilly?"

Forcing a polite smile at his attempt at wit, Leigh started the car's engine and followed Scenic Road to Ocean Avenue and so to downtown. He was just another client, after all, and the more fool she for ever thinking otherwise. One had meals and drinks with clients; one was nice to them. It was part of her job, part of what they paid for, buyer or seller.

And now that he was nothing more than a client, Leigh had no trouble at all asking him in a straightforward way, "Are you married, Mr. Madigan?"

Dow didn't even turn to face her; on the contrary, he turned his head away to gaze out the side window. In measured tones that bore the weight of some heavy emotion—just which, Leigh couldn't tell—he replied, "No, Miss Mallory, I am not." Then he laughed, a harsh, scornful sound. "Your precious beach will go up in flames before *I* take a wife."

So now she knew; and obviously Minnie was right. There was pain in his remarks, but whatever caused it was none of Leigh's business, and she'd do well, as Minnie said, to "stay away from this one." And putting it mildly, Dow Madigan's difficult and prickly personality would make that easy.

Leigh took Dow to La Marmite, a small, charming

café on San Carlos, decorated in the French country manner. A congenial buzz of happy diners welcomed them as they entered the small room and waited for a table. The white walls were hung with simply framed Lautrec posters and prints by Monet and Renoir. Hundreds of bottles of wine were displayed on the long wooden rack that ran the length of the room, dividing it in half, small tables on one side, and a long banquette upholstered in flowered tapestry cloth along the other wall. Wooden shutters softened the bright midday light, making the intimate little room the more so.

A fresh-faced local girl dressed in a blue-and-white gingham dress, her hair done in braids coiled around her head, showed them to a cozy corner table tucked away under the stairwell.

When Dow had given the drinks order to the girl, he settled back against the padded bench and seemed to relax. "Your Miss Wanamaker is quite a character," he said when their drinks were served. "Was that really a voodoo doll she had in her hand?" A skeptical smile played about his mouth.

Ever since Leigh herself had met Minnie, she'd enjoyed watching the startled reactions of any stranger introduced to her, but now Leigh felt no desire to enter into any amused conjecture about her in some ways outré friend. Dow had spoiled even that small, innocent pleasure. Anyone who saw the Pacific Ocean as "pretty" couldn't begin to properly appreciate Minnie Wanamaker. Leigh replied flatly, discouragingly, "I don't really know. It may have been; or it may just have been a doll she's making for one of her grandchildren."

Dow laughed incredulously. "Do you mean to tell me that bizarre woman is a grandmother?"

Stung, Leigh responded against her will to what she felt as an insult to Minnie. "We do have grandmothers in California, you know." And then, for the second time that day, Leigh cursed her stupid, bungling tongue.

As she'd known he would, as soon as the words were out of her mouth, Dow pounced on them. "Why, so you do! It *slipped my mind* for just a moment, you see, but now I remember. Not grandmothers like you'd find in the rest of the country, of course—some of you have bizarre grandmothers and some of you even have *famous* grandmothers."

Even though Dow's manner was somewhere between a mean tease and a friendly kidding, Leigh instantly leaped to the offensive. Fixing Dow with a hard glare, she demanded, "Why do you keep harping on that? What is so important about a simple memory slip that you persist in bringing it up?"

To Leigh's great surprise, the teasing smile rapidly left Dow's face, to be replaced by a look of—could it be?—conciliation. When he answered her, there was a note of apology in his voice. "You're right. I'm being a bore about that. I'm sorry. As a matter of fact, ever since we left the beach I've had the distinct feeling that I owe you an apology for something. If you'll tell me what it is, I'll be glad to oblige."

Leigh didn't know how to respond to this new facet of Dow's personality. It was quite like seeing a rampaging wolf suddenly turn into a poodle puppy. What was even more amazing, she realized she really didn't like to see him this way: she didn't like to see him . . . well, humbled. Pushing this silly notion out of her mind, she maintained her stance of cool reserve. "Don't be absurd, Mr. Madigan. You owe me nothing."

A smile flickered around his mouth. "Ah, it's like that, is it? If I don't know, then you're not going to tell me. Very well, then; will you settle for a blanket apology?"

Frowning in great concentration, Leigh studied the menu. "The veal is very nice here. So are the sweetbreads."

"I see," Dow said, a dangerous note creeping back into his voice. "It must be a specific apology, but I must guess the offense. Is that it?"

Ignoring his question, Leigh said, "Or, if you prefer seafood, the salmon is fresh here, and they serve a very nice coquille St. Jacques."

Dow drained the last of his martini. "Let me guess, then," he said. "You're angry because I didn't whip out my checkbook and buy that house right then and there?"

Leigh sniffed, not deigning to answer.

"No," he said thoughtfully, "I didn't think it could be that." Then, in a wondering tone, as if asking himself more than Leigh, he said, "Could it have anything to do with my not being married?"

"Please, Mr. Madigan," Leigh said with weary scorn, "wouldn't you like to order—?"

Interrupting her fiercely, Dow demanded, "Stop calling me Mr. Madigan!"

Several diners raised their heads to peer at the table in the corner, and Dow lowered his voice to a grim, unpleasant pitch and continued. "I think I've got it. It's got something to do with what I said about the view, hasn't it?"

When Leigh refused to reply or respond in any way at all, Dow sat back against the bench, satisfaction plain on his face. "So that's it. A case of 'love me, love my ocean.'"

When phrased that way, Dow's correct guess so embarrassed Leigh that she felt herself flush. She said crisply, "Don't be ridiculous!"

The two of them locked eyes, Dow with a smug, sarcastic smile and Leigh looking back at him with a defiant, mulishly stubborn set to her chin.

"You Californians are incredible," Dow said softly. "You think everything out here in this insane state is the best, don't you? Even your *ocean* is better than the Atlantic, isn't it?"

Leigh lowered her eyes and said primly, "I'm sure the Atlantic Ocean is very nice, in its own way."

Dow emitted a great gust of exasperation. "Nice!" he cried. "Nice! And I suppose this restaurant is 'nicer' than anything in New York City?"

Leigh said coolly, "I'm sure you have lovely French restaurants in New York City, too—if you can find one where the waiters aren't rude."

"Oh, of course," he said with heavy sarcasm, "every waiter in California is *nice*. And I suppose Sam Nelson is a much *nicer* man than *I* am, too."

Leigh stared at Dow as if he'd truly gone mad. Why on earth should he bring Sam Nelson into what was already a conversation straight out of *Alice in Wonderland*, so incredible was it. By now, the two of them were the center of attention, and from the corner of her eye Leigh saw that the maître d' was hovering nearby, ready to spring into action if necessary.

In a low voice, Leigh said warningly, "Mr. Madigan, you're making a spectacle of yourself, you're disturbing people, please control yourself."

In a scornful tone, Dow said, "God forbid that anything unpleasant should happen in Carmel. You know what your trouble is? You're hedonists, all of you. You're all so besotted with ease and beauty that you're not even fit to live in the real world!"

Leigh, nearly faint with mortification now, pushed back her chair, preparing to get up and walk out, leaving this maniac to rave on alone. But as she arose, Dow shoved the small table aside, threw some money on it, and followed her as she wove through the tables full of interested diners toward the door. Dow had fallen silent, but Leigh felt his menacing presence close on her heels, like a land mine threatening to explode at the merest misstep. As she walked past the maître d' she said hurriedly, "I'm so sorry, monsieur, very sorry. . . ."

The maître d', a look of concern on his Gallic face, murmured, "If there's been some fault in the service . . . ?"

"Not at all," Leigh reassured him hastily, "the service was lovely, as always. It's just that"—she gestured behind her to a glowering Dow—"the gentleman is from New York City."

"Ahhh," the maître d' breathed, closing his eyes briefly in understanding.

When Leigh and Dow were outside in the shady little brick courtyard, she turned on him and said frigidly, "As Mr. Kipling once so aptly said, 'East is East, and West is West, and never the twain shall meet.' Our association is finished as of now, Mr. Madigan. I strongly advise you to forget your plans to buy a house in Carmel—indeed, in *any* part of this state. But if you persist, you'll have to find another broker to work with."

Dow's face was pale from some ravaging emotion, his voice ragged as he answered, "That's the first sensible thing I've heard you say since I had the misfortune to bumble into your office, Miss Mallory. You may rest assured that I won't trouble you again."

Then he turned on his heel and stalked away toward Ocean Avenue, leaving Leigh to stand there and watch him until he blended into the crowds on the street and disappeared from her life as if he'd been only a dream.

Chapter Five

The next morning, the last Saturday of November, Leigh went downtown to accomplish a task that for the first time in her life was a chore rather than a delight. Christmas was neither in the air nor in Leigh's heart, but it was evident in the stores of Carmel and well within shopping distance on the calendar. If gifts were to reach her mother and stepfather in West Germany, they must be mailed by next Monday.

The day was overcast, the air damp and chill with the oppressive threat of rain, yet the crowded shops were stifling. The merchandise all seemed either too expensive or shoddy; the right sizes were in the wrong colors, the right colors in the wrong materials—everything grated on Leigh's nerves.

At last she settled on a Dunhill pipe for her

stepfather and gathered up her parcels to head for Pamela's shop. If she couldn't find something for her mother among her friend's choice merchandise, she'd give up and make Dibbie take over the chore. It wouldn't hurt that flighty creature to do her fair share for a change, Leigh thought grumpily.

It was quiet in the small, intimate shop, and the rich fragrance of expensive perfume in the air soothed Leigh's tension headache somewhat. Surprised to be the only customer in such a popular shop, Leigh was idly stroking a display pile of cashmere sweaters from Scotland when Pamela entered through the swinging louvered doors that separated the back office from the sales area.

"Leigh! I'm so glad to see you! Isn't it a dismal day?"

Leigh turned to see the pretty, cheerful face of her softly rounded friend. Not for Pamela a diet of carrot sticks and celery. She professed to believe that men preferred a woman with plenty of hills and valleys and curves, like an interesting racecourse, and her warm and generous nature guaranteed that her beliefs came true. It was never Pamela who went to concerts or plays unescorted or sat at home on weekend nights with only the television for company. Only in her late twenties, Pamela was already a tradition among her Carmel contemporaries: if you're down in the dumps, call Pam; she'll cheer you up.

Perhaps it was this loving quality that made her say, after seeing Leigh's pinched, tense expression, "On a day like this, I could kill for a French pastry.

Why don't I close up this joint and we'll go to the *patisserie* for some goodies and a nice cup of tea."

Protesting that she had to get her Christmas shopping done, Leigh let herself be marched out of the shop toward Mission Street and the comfort of the pretty blue-and-white tea shop where tired shoppers often revived themselves with dreamy confections and a cup of tea or a glass of sherry. After they'd chosen what Pamela considered an ample supply of pastries from the bakery counter, they took the table in front of the fireplace, alight with a small, friendly fire on this damp, chilly day.

"There, now," Pamela said, sighing with pleasure, "isn't this better?"

"But aren't you worried you'll lose business by closing up the shop so close to Christmas?" Leigh asked.

Pamela shrugged, taking a luscious mouthful of a succulent Napoleon. "Life's too short to worry about trifles."

Leigh smiled at this typical Carmel attitude. It was ten-forty-five in the morning and there were several other Carmel shopkeepers in the tearoom, indulging in the custom of taking a coffee break whenever the impulse struck. Leigh smiled grimly as it occurred to her what Dow Madigan would make of such "hedonistic" behavior. It was an everyday occurrence to find a penciled note taped to a shop door, reading "Back at eleven" or "Gone to the beach, back at three." And as casual as things were now, even so they were much more regulated than in the old laissez-faire days Gran loved to tell about. In the early Carmel days, when the village was populated only by the original artist settlers, shopkeepers left their stores not only unattended but also unlocked, with the understanding that customers would come in, take what they wanted, and leave payment in boxes left on the counter for that purpose.

"Besides," Pamela went on, "thanks to you, early this morning one customer bought enough stuff to pay my whole month's rent."

"Thanks to me? What do you mean?" Leigh asked.

"Surely you know who I mean, Leigh. How many incredibly gorgeous strangers have you sent to my shop lately?"

"Oh. Him. It just slipped my mind for a moment that he'd asked me about women's clothing shops," Leigh muttered, annoyed that once again the man's impact on her had turned her mind to a sieve.

"Anyway, I'm in your debt," Pamela said. "He bought enough clothes to outfit a Lady Godiva, from the skin out."

Leigh stared morosely into her cup of tea and pushed a delicate flake of pastry around on the blue-and-white china plate. "Lucky her," she said sarcastically. "He may be good-looking, but he's certainly a pill."

"A *pill*? Maybe you *have* sent more than one man to my shop. We can't be talking about the same one. *This* one was a charmer." Then Pamela grinned wickedly. "In fact, the answer to a maiden's prayer."

A stab of jealousy surprised Leigh, and ashamed of herself, she immediately squelched it. If her dear friend Pamela thought Dow Madigan was the answer to a prayer, then more power to her. One woman's meat was another woman's poison. As far as Leigh was concerned, Mr. Supercilious Arrogance was more like a *curse* from God than the answer to a prayer.

Licking her fingertips daintily and selecting a pastry covered with chocolate shot, Pamela said thoughtfully, "However, this lucky woman, one Elaine Stanley by name, is three thousand miles away in New York and this delicious man is right here in little old Carmel. Surely there's got to be some advantage just in proximity alone."

How annoying it was that everyone but Leigh— oh, yes, and Minnie—was so thoroughly taken in by Dow Madigan's surface charm. Her own loved ones at home, and now one of her best friends, all thought this sour, unpleasant creature was a man of charm, culture, and good breeding. Perhaps without the benefit of Minnie's deeply seeing eye, even Leigh herself might've briefly succumbed to his undeniable good looks. But they were right, Minnie and Leigh, and Pamela's recent news proved it yet again: Dow Madigan was a man to stay away from for more reasons than one.

In spite of her indifference to Dow Madigan's affairs, just to keep the conversation going, Leigh casually asked, "How do you happen to know the name of the woman he bought the clothes for? Did he talk to you about her?"

Pamela scrutinized Leigh. "No, he asked me if I'd mail the packages for him, so naturally he gave me her name and address. Elaine Stanley, something-something Park Avenue, New York City."

"Pamela!" Leigh laughingly protested. "I don't care what her address is."

"Do you want to know exactly what he bought?" Pamela asked slyly.

"No, you nut," Leigh replied, not meeting Pam's eyes as she drank the last of her tea.

Pam nodded gravely. "Of course you don't. Who cares what he does, since he's such a terrible pill."

Leigh had agreed to spend Sunday with Sam Nelson and his children, up from the city for the weekend. That morning she gave more thought to her clothes than she usually did when she went out with Sam. They were just friends, but even so, it wouldn't hurt her to do him the courtesy of dressing up a bit.

Because the day's activities were bound to be rugged, she chose a pair of wide-wale corduroy pants in a camel color and the new butterscotch turtleneck cashmere sweater she'd bought yesterday, just like the lavender one she'd selected for her mother's Christmas gift. Leigh tied a silk scarf in shades of tans and grays around her throat and put on a pair of crepe-soled walking shoes. The day was just crisp enough to require a jacket, and her dark brown suede blazer would do very well.

When Leigh walked into the sitting room to wait for Sam, she found Annie Channing sitting at her noble old Bechstein piano playing one of Mendelssohn's *Songs Without Words*. John sat near the lit fire wrestling with the enormous crossword puzzle in the Sunday San Francisco *Chronicle*.

"Where's everybody else?" Leigh asked John quietly, so as not to disturb the lovely music.

John ticked off on his fingers the whereabouts of every other resident of Illyria. "Dibbie got in after two o'clock last night, so she's still asleep. Burt's in charge of the Adult Discussion group at church today and won't be home until noon. Your grandmother is in her rooms dressing to go out."

Leigh noticed the coolness of that "your grandmother" instead of the usual warm "dear Jane" or "your Gran." Something had pushed John's sensitive nose out of joint.

"Where's she going?" Leigh asked, never doubting that John would know.

With obvious pique he replied, "I have no idea."

Hoping to cajole him back to his usual sunny state, Leigh smiled conspiratorially. "Very mysterious."

"I'm sure she has a right to her privacy," he replied snappishly. "No need for her to act as if I was prying."

Before Leigh could consider this new domestic development, the old-fashioned doorbell pealed and she said over her shoulder, "I'll get it, John; that'll be Sam."

But there stood Dow Madigan, so tall he filled the doorway, with a gift-wrapped package in his hands. He must have seen the shock on Leigh's face, for a slight sardonic smile lifted the corners of his mouth as he drawled, "We've got to stop meeting like this."

Leigh blushed furiously, both at his sarcastic words and at the leap of joy she felt at the sight

73

of him. "I didn't . . . I wasn't expecting to see you . . ." she stammered.

"Nor I you," he replied coolly. "I have an engagement with Miss Parnell. Perhaps bad memory runs in the family and she forgot to mention it."

Angry tears suddenly stung Leigh's eyes, but she was saved from the further embarrassment of having Dow see them when she heard footsteps behind her in the foyer and turned her head to see Gran sailing toward them, her hands outstretched in welcome, her face wreathed in smiles. John Channing hovered in the doorway between the foyer and the sitting room, his round blue eyes back to normal now, bright with curiosity.

"My dear boy, do come in while I gather my wraps," Gran said in a warm, indulgent voice.

Leigh fell back as Dow stepped forward into the foyer and with a courtly little bow presented the package to Gran. On many a gift-giving occasion, Leigh had enjoyed Gran's masterful performance of receiving and opening gifts. She removed wrappings neatly with nimble and delicate movements of her slender fingers, interspersed with little cries and coos of pleasure, curiosity, and gratitude, giving even the most humble of gifts the status of tribute to a head of state.

This time was no exception, and in spite of herself, Leigh watched with fascination, along with Dow and John, as Gran lifted from the heavy, glossy white paper a white satin five-pound box of Godiva chocolates. This absolute ultimate in candy, Leigh knew, was in a class with Russian caviar and truffles from France.

And at the sight of the illustrious name Godiva on the elegant white box, Leigh's lip curled with disdain as she was reminded that only yesterday Dow Madigan had courted yet another woman with expensive gifts.

"What a heavenly treat!" Gran cried. "We'll all enjoy them so much. Leigh's mad for chocolates, aren't you, dear?"

"Actually, Gran, I never touch candy," Leigh said. "You must be confusing me with Dibbie."

Just then Leigh saw Sam's car pull up in front of the house. "Here's darling Sam, I must run." She bent to kiss Gran's cheek and in a low but perfectly audible voice confided, "I may be *very* late, darling, so don't wait up for me. I'll see you in the morning." Then, with a breezy, carefree smile, Leigh ran out the door like any young woman eager to be alone with that special man.

The first three days of the following week were very busy ones for both Leigh and Dibbie. On Monday and Tuesday both young women had spent much of the day at various title companies in the village, steering several buyers and sellers through the final flurry of paper signing that marked the close of escrow. Today, Wednesday, they'd risen at six A.M. to make the drive into San Francisco to attend a real estate seminar on tax-deferred property exchanges.

Leigh was grateful that not since Sunday morning had she seen or heard of Dow Madigan, except for Monday morning at breakfast when Gran had given Leigh a full report on the brunch Dow treated her to at the Highlands Inn, where he was staying. It wasn't until after dinner on Wednesday evening that Dow was once again forced on Leigh's attention.

Four of the five card players sat in Illyria's sitting room waiting for Gran so the weekly poker game could begin. Burt looked up from *The Wall Street Journal* and said to John Channing, "Madigan-Stanley Pharmaceuticals is down five points, John. Didn't I tell you I smelled trouble?"

"So you did, Burt," John said admiringly. "And I never suspected a thing."

Leigh asked, "What's this?"

"Well, John, when you've traveled in the business world as long as I did, you learn to read between the lines. Just a few little comments Dow made last Sunday . . . I put two and two together."

"What's wrong?" Leigh asked.

"Poor dear boy," Annie Channing murmured, "I do hope it isn't serious."

"Is something wrong?" Leigh asked more loudly.

Burt pursed his mouth thoughtfully. "I wonder if it's this Stanley fellow who's making waves."

"Who's Stanley?" Leigh asked, thinking the name was familiar. Wasn't that the name of the woman Dow had sent gifts to?

"I'll tell all my friends to buy more Placid-eeze," Annie said determinedly. "Isn't that the name of Dow's aspirin?"

"What aspirin? What are you all talking about?" Leigh demanded loudly.

"Dow's *business,* dear," Annie said impatiently, as to a pesky, nagging child.

John sighed. "As if the poor fellow didn't have

76

enough on his plate right now, what with his grandfather's death and all."

"But he's a sharp one," Burt said. "He's been running that business since his mid-twenties, you know. He said he was thirty-seven, so that's nearly fifteen years he's been in charge. No slouch could have managed a huge concern like that for so long."

"Slouch!" Annie said defensively. "Who on earth said dear Dow was a slouch?"

"No one, dearest," John said to her kindly. "Burt and I were saying just the opposite."

"I should think so! He's a wonderful young man. I just wonder," Annie mused, "why he's never married. They must have very inept girls in the east. He won't last a year if he stays out here." At this last remark Annie threw Leigh a significant glance that said plainer than words: A word to the wise is sufficient.

Not deigning to respond in any way to Annie's silly remark, Leigh kept a pinched-mouth silence. It was sickening, really, to hear them all extolling that awful man's many virtues! Poor fellow! Dear boy! So sharp, so smart, so wonderful! Little did they know—and yet, they all took his side against her, Leigh thought furiously, her very own family!

And how did they come to know all those things, anyway? How had they come to be so intimate with him, while she . . . ? It was really too much to be made to feel like the deceived wife in the legendary triangle—the stupid, trusting wife always the last to know. And just who was doing the deceiving around here, anyway—Dow Madigan or her very own family?

If they knew what she knew—well, why shouldn't she tell them what a bounder he really was! Leigh's rankling heart overflowed into a burst of speech just as Gran swept into the room and gracefully took her seat at the card table.

"You all wouldn't think he was such a paragon of virtue if you'd heard the scene he caused at La Marmite last Friday. I was so mortified I nearly died!" Leigh cried.

The others drifted to the card table, leaving Leigh in the middle of the room alone. Gran said in a brisk, no-nonsense voice, "We heard that story days ago. Mrs. Benton-Anderson was there, and she said you were being very rude to Dow, sitting there like a sphinx while he tried to make conversation. I do deplore that sullen streak of yours, Leigh. You certainly didn't get that from my side of the family."

"Gran!" Leigh beseeched.

"Come sit down now, darling. You're making a mountain out of a molehill. I think you're overtired from your trip to the city today," Gran said imperturbably.

"Perhaps I *am,*" Leigh cried passionately. "Yes, I definitely am! I think I'll just go up to my room and go to bed," she said spitefully, knowing full well that a threat to spoil the poker game would bring them all around to her side again.

So shocked was Leigh then, when Gran merely nodded absently, that tears of frustration and defeat filled her eyes, and her voice was choked with tears as she said hesitantly, "Well, then . . . good night, I guess. . . ."

"Darling, before you go, could you just do me one small favor?"

"Certainly, Gran," Leigh said eagerly, hoping for a chance to save face and join them after all. The last thing in the world she wanted was to be by herself, to think and brood.

"Go give Dow a call, there's a good child, and ask him to join us for Sunday dinner," Gran said casually, shuffling the deck for the first hand.

Leigh caught her breath and her eyes narrowed in anger. "I certainly will not! You all think he's so wonderful, one of you can call him. I'm going to bed!" and she turned on her heel.

She heard Gran's voice say confidentially to the others, "You see how stubborn she is?" and then louder, to Leigh, she said with that sweetly martyred tone Leigh was helpless against, "You're absolutely right, my dear. I'm just a selfish, thoughtless, demanding old woman. I'll do it myself as soon as I catch my breath and my knee stops aching. Or perhaps John or Burt will help me out. But you run along to bed now . . . and forgive your old Gran for being such a burden to you in her old age."

Leigh sighed gustily and raised closed eyes to heaven. Turning to face them all, she said wearily, "All right, I surrender, Gran. What time shall I ask him to come?"

Gran smiled sweetly. "Around five, don't you think?"

But, scant moments later, when Leigh returned to the sitting room and Persia Parnell saw her grand-daughter's white face, her hurt eyes brimming with tears, all games and power plays were set aside. Gran rose abruptly from her chair and hurried to put her arms around Leigh. "What is it, darling?" she asked with frightened concern.

"He's gone," Leigh replied in a stunned tone. "They said he's . . . just gone! He left Monday morning with no forwarding address," she said on a rising note of anguish that cracked at the top. Then Leigh sank down on the nearest chair, put her white face into her hands, and began to sob.

"Leigh, dearest, don't cry—why are you crying?" Gran asked, alarmed.

"It's all my fault, it's all my fault," Leigh moaned.

"Poor darling," Annie fussed, fluttering at Leigh's side.

"But he didn't even say good-bye . . . oh, how could he?" Leigh wept.

Burt said gruffly, "Don't take on so, little one. I'm sure he'll get in touch with you soon, he'll explain, you'll see."

"Of course he will," John echoed, patting Leigh's hand.

Wailing now, Leigh shook her head vehemently. "No, no, you don't understand! It's Gran I'm crying for, she cares so much for him. I know he hates *me,* but how could he do this to her? How could he do this to *Gran?*"

As one, four heads in varying shades of gray lifted their faces from Leigh, hunched so miserably in the chair, and exchanged a look of sympathy for the weeping young woman. But then, starting with Gran, one by one, each soft, wrinkled face took on a new expression—a sly, knowing, triumphant smile.

Chapter Six

"I hope you're feeling better this morning, dear," Gran said solicitously as she sat with Leigh at the breakfast table.

"I told you, Gran," Leigh said patiently, "I was only thinking of you. If I overreacted a bit, it was only because I was tired from the seminar, as you yourself pointed out."

Gran hastily agreed. "Of course, I quite understand that, and it's very good and kind of you to be so concerned with my feelings. But then, you've always been a softhearted child, in spite of that facade of reserve you maintain."

Leigh nibbled listlessly on a slice of toasted raisin bread spread with pomegranate jelly. "I don't know how softhearted I am, but I'm glad you're taking his incredibly rude disappearance so well."

Fiddling idly with the tendrils of pink fuchsia in

the Waterford vase on the table, Gran said lightly, "Oh, well, it's just that I feel sure there's a good explanation for his departure. Perhaps he was called out of town unexpectedly on business. Whatever, I'm sure he'll be in touch soon."

"What's wrong with his business, anyway?" Leigh asked, remembering the mysterious conversation between John and Burt last night. Not that she cared, of course.

"Oh, heavens, I wouldn't know," Gran said, taking refuge in feminine ignorance of worldly affairs. "I just know that no grandson of Dow Madigan would leave town without saying good-bye to those who'd befriended him. That sort of thing just isn't done," she said with finality.

Pouring herself another cup of coffee, Leigh smiled wryly at Gran. "I don't doubt that *your* Dow Madigan was a wonderful man, Gran, but I think you count too much on heredity. My Dow . . . I mean, *this* Dow Madigan is, not to put too fine a point on it, a stinker."

Gran sighed. "Funny how different you and Deborah are. Now, if it were Deborah that Dow was inter . . . well, had come into contact with, we'd all be making wedding plans. In fact, I'd bet on it."

"Oh, Gran," Leigh said with exasperation. "It's been just exactly one week since any of us clapped eyes on him, and here you've got him married to one of us. What is it with you and marriage, anyway!" she cried. "I'd think after five failed marriages of your own, you'd give up on the whole institution."

Gran looked at her granddaughter with astonishment. "But, Leigh, it's because I do think so much of the institution that I married five times! It's not the fault of marriage that mine never worked out, it was the fault of the people involved," and here her voice fell, "mostly my fault, I have to admit."

Leigh searched Gran's face. Seldom did the older woman refer to her personal past. When she reminisced, it was almost always about her career and her friends, now mostly dead and gone.

"How so, Gran?" Leigh asked gently, not wanting to pry but suddenly needing very much to know how her grandmother thought she'd failed.

Gran's eyes grew shadowy as she looked into the distant past, and her voice took on a note of careful consideration as she began to talk. "For one thing, when I married your grandfather, I was a very spoiled, silly young girl. I took everything he gave me for granted, all the love, the pride in my talent, all the encouragement to grow and develop— everything. I took it all and thought it was simply my due. I didn't see until . . . oh, years and years later what a priceless gift it'd all been.

"He was a good many years older than I, and his maturity enabled him to put up with quite a lot of foolishness from me. But eventually—I suppose when he saw that I showed no signs of growing up—he left me for a woman who understood the value of what he had to give and who was willing to give the best of herself in return."

Gran looked at Leigh with shimmering eyes. "You and Dibbie don't remember him, do you?"

"Just dimly," Leigh replied quietly. "He died when we were so young, and we saw him so seldom."

Gran sighed. "Such a shame. Well, from that point on, Leigh, it was pretty much downhill. I'd liked being married, you see." Gran laughed shortly. "And why not? I'd been cosseted and indulged, had everything my way—anyone would like 'marriage' who saw it as I did, as a one-way street or a chest full of treasures for the taking. So, very soon I married again. But for years, out of resentment and hurt pride, I blamed your grandfather for the failure of that first marriage, and subconsciously, I think now, never again let myself get into a position where I could be humiliated."

Gran shook her head in wonder at how blind she'd been. "Of course, I blamed each of my husbands in turn for the failure of each subsequent marriage. It wasn't until after the fifth one that I finally realized it was I who was lacking. And by then it was too late for me to really love a man properly."

"But, Gran," Leigh protested, "you had several love affairs after the last divorce. Why do you say it was too late?"

Gran smiled knowingly. "A successful love affair is quite different from a good marriage, Leigh. It's like the difference between being a baby-sitter and being a parent. Love is very like any other talent or ability; if it isn't used, it atrophies. After all those years of living with a shell around my heart to keep it invulnerable from pain, one day I realized that the shell had *become* my heart." Gran took Leigh's hand in hers. "I don't want to see that happen to you, my dear child."

Leigh's eyes filled with tears. How could this best of all women believe she didn't have a loving heart?

"Don't you think, after all these years, that Dibbie and I would know if you had a shell for a heart, Gran? You're more capable of love than anyone else I know. More than you know yourself."

Gran smiled faintly and patted Leigh's hand. "Maybe so, my dear girl. But if I am, then so are you, Leigh—more than *you* know."

Gran's words hovered in Leigh's mind over the next few uneventful days, coming back at odd times as she delivered a deed of trust to the recorder's office, made Xerox copies of new-listing sheets at the title company, called lenders to check on the latest interest rates, or, like now, sat watching the rain drizzle down outside her office window.

"Thank God it's Friday," Dibbie said, peering into her compact mirror, pushing with irritation at her curls, made kinky by the moisture in the air.

"Most real estate people consider Friday the beginning of the busiest part of their week, Deborah," Leigh said pointedly.

"Only if they have nothing better to do," Dibbie replied, snapping her compact shut and tossing it into her leather shoulder bag. "Only if they're compulsive, driven workaholics," she added with a teasing grin, "or if they have to support a family. I'd rather devote my weekends to finding someone to support *me*."

Leigh laughed shortly. "Gran thinks one of us should've snagged Dow Madigan before he got away. And considering what I think of him, it would've had to be you, Dib. How would that strike you?"

Dibbie hesitated, then said, "Whatever else I may be, dear sister, I'm not a poacher. Dow Madigan's off limits, already spoken for."

Not surprised at the efficiency of the Carmel grapevine, Leigh said, "Oh, Pamela told you, then."

Again Dibbie hesitated; then, "Yes, Pamela. She did mention it."

As if to herself, Leigh said softly, "Actually, that's where *I* think he went. A business trip wouldn't keep him from saying good-bye . . ." She trailed off into silence.

Tentatively Dibbie asked, "You think he went to see Pamela?"

Leigh looked at Dibbie with surprise. "Of course not. I said I think he went back to New York to see the woman he loves. You know, his partner's daughter—Elaine Stanley. Or"—Leigh frowned in thought—"at least I think she must be his partner's daughter."

"Well, if he did," Dibbie said, looking out the window of the office, "he's back now."

A great blaze of hope leaped up in Leigh's heart as the old pharmacy bell above the door jingled brightly and Dow Madigan entered the office. His expression was as overcast and dour as the day he so miraculously came out of.

"Well, well, speak of the devil and he shall appear," Dibbie teased. "My sister was just talking about you, Dow."

Dow managed a pained smile and said dryly, "I thought I felt my ears burning."

"I was not! Deborah . . ." Leigh warned, anxious lest Dibbie would expand further on their recent discussion, even going so far as to ask Dow where he'd been.

"Never fear, sister, I'm on my way out." Dibbie gathered up her handbag and her jacket, and pausing at the office door, said, "Oh, about that matter we were discussing, Leigh—try to be more careful this time. Gran won't like it if you botch it up again."

Now that Dibbie's distracting and volatile presence was gone, Leigh recovered herself enough to notice an exhausted slope to Dow's shoulders that she'd never seen before. As she scrutinized him more closely, she saw also a tense whiteness around his mouth and shadows of strain or fatigue staining the delicate skin under his eyes. Why, he looked actually sick, she thought with a pang.

"Are you ill, Dow?" she asked, concerned. "You look terrible."

He managed a weak, sickly smile as he sank down onto one of the clients' chairs. "You, on the other hand, look ravishing, as always."

She briefly looked down at the cinnamon wool gored skirt and the copper silk blouse she'd worn that morning and saw nothing ravishing about either of them.

Letting this unconvincing compliment go unacknowledged, Leigh thought with fleeting irony how much more congenial Dow seemed when he was ill than when he was well. But concern for him, as for any suffering creature, kept her from replying with anything but gentleness.

"Is there anything I can do for you? Would you like an aspirin or a cup of tea?"

"I'm all right," he answered in a voice that belied his words. "I've just had several very unpleasant days in the city."

So Burt was right, Leigh thought. And now she remembered that when she'd met Dow he'd said something about opening a new branch of his business on the west coast.

"Business problems can be very difficult," she said sympathetically.

Dow shook his head wearily. "It wasn't business, it was family trouble."

"Oh," Leigh said, taken aback. "I'm sorry, I didn't mean to pry—I didn't know you had any family out here."

Dow moved restlessly, as if to shake some heavy burden from his shoulders. "I don't, except for my soon-to-be-ex-brother-in-law. He's been giving the whole family a very hard time lately, and when I was informed that he'd shown up in San Francisco, I took the opportunity to straighten him out on a few matters," Dow said grimly.

"I see," Leigh murmured. After only a week's acquaintance with Dow she could well imagine how he would "straighten out" anyone so rash as to get on the wrong side of him.

It wasn't lost on Leigh that here was yet another example of love gone awry. On Leigh's mental ledger of romance there was one marriage on the credit side—John and Annie Channing's—and many, many others outweighing theirs on the debit side. In spite of Gran's cautionary words that one must be open to love, in spite of her gallantry in taking the blame for the failure of all five of her marriages, the fact remained that much more often than not, love ended—and ended in wreckage, pain, and humiliation. In the face of these facts, it hardly mattered *whose* fault it was.

With the effort of an exhausted man, Dow rose from the chair and held his hand out toward Leigh. "Come. We're going to visit Tor House. We have an appointment at four o'clock, and it's nearly that now."

"But . . ." Leigh automatically protested, and then, some gentler part of her unwilling to aggravate Dow's frazzled state, she stood up at his command, locked up the office, and ventured out with Dow into the wet, gloomy day.

With a light but firm hand on Leigh's elbow, Dow steered her down the street a half-block to where his silvery gray Mercedes sedan was parked. He settled her into the sinfully comfortable seat upholstered in cordovan leather and closed the passenger door with that quietly authoritative click of the well-made, expensive automobile.

Dow drove as Leigh might've imagined he would—with efficiency and speed just moderate enough to be legal. Since he seemed to know where he was going, Leigh offered no directions or advice. Instead, she said with some hesitancy, "Gran will be glad to know you're back."

"Oh, she knows it," he said offhandedly. "I called her when I got in this morning."

"I see," Leigh said. She was glad, of course, that Dow had behaved properly toward an elderly woman who was fond of him. "I suppose it was Gran who suggested you take me along to Tor House?" Leigh asked dryly.

Dow turned to look at Leigh, his right eyebrow raised. "What odd ideas you have. Do I seem to you the kind of person who requires an entertainment director?" he said shortly.

Odd ideas, indeed! Leigh bristled—but silently. She *must* have "odd ideas" to find herself going *sightseeing,* of all things, with this exasperating man that just last Friday she'd so ardently wished never to see again. What was *wrong* with her that she'd veered from total repugnance to total submission— just because he seemed a bit down-at-the-mouth! But try as she would, Leigh found it impossible to maintain any indignation or animosity toward Dow today; so, like the sensible girl she was, she gave it up and sat silently at his side until they reached their destination.

Dow maneuvered through the narrow, meandering streets of the neighborhood above the beach until they reached Tor House, nestled on the cliff that overhung Scenic Road, the two-lane highway that paralleled the beach. Once, in the halcyon days of Carmel's infancy as a sparsely settled artists' colony, this cottage stood alone here on the cliff overlooking the limitless expanse of the Pacific Ocean. Now it was one more house, albeit a special and revered one, on a street of other prestigious houses.

Dow and Leigh entered on foot through the low stone wall that separated everyday life from the poet's enchanted cottage by the sea. Tor House and

Hawk Tower, surrounded as if in a meadow, by charmingly blowsy gardens in the English manner, looked not as if they'd been built by the hands of men, but as if they were natural stone outcroppings heaved up from the rich, sandy loam beneath them. Built of gray and weathered stone hauled up the cliff from the beach below by Jeffers himself, they looked akin to the rugged, primitive stone cottages on the wild English coast that were their inspiration. Tor House, built over a span of years by Jeffers and local laborers, its slow growth determined by limitations of time and money, was actually a series of small cottages tied together by the unifying element of the stone.

Off to the left of the brick path that led to the house, an exuberant herb garden flourished, the cheerful borage blooming blue and pennyroyal creeping onto the path to soften their steps and release its pungent peppermint aroma as they walked. A small rose garden filled the area in front of the cottage's heavy wooden door, an ancient Roman cupid posing coyly in its center, and sweet alyssum covering the ground around it.

When the pleasant woman in her mid-thirties, a docent for the historical society, opened the door to greet them, Leigh saw the subtle expansion of the woman's eyes when she first saw Dow Madigan and ushered them into the tiny entrance foyer.

Leigh stood to one side waiting while Dow paid the modest sum charged for touring the house and tower and signed the guest book. As she watched his dark head bent over the leather-bound book, and watched the other woman gaze at him raptly, Leigh became aware of an unfamiliar emotion gathering strength within her. It seemed to have to do with being escorted by a man so virile and magnetic that the very sight of him widened another woman's eyes. But could it be only that? Leigh questioned herself. Could it be such a base and unworthy emotion as that she felt? And when Dow straightened and put his hand possessively on Leigh's shoulder, saying, "Come along, now, Leigh," she felt a little shudder of delight curl up her spine.

"We'll begin with the tower," Mrs. Welling said, preceding Dow out the door they'd just entered by.

As Leigh followed, she glanced down at the guest book and saw Dow's name above her own, written in a bold, flaring script. Then, beside their names, in the "Comments" column, where others had written such things as "lovely," "charming," "inspiring," she read something that made her heart ache with some unidentifiable emotion. Dow had written: "Some lucky day each November . . ."

The tower wasn't far from the house, and small as towers go, only forty feet high. Jeffers had built it as a retreat for his beloved wife, Una; and perhaps because it was intended for her solitude, the steep outer stairway didn't encourage easy access. Although Dow, with his long, male-strong legs, wasn't daunted, there was no way for a woman to gracefully ascend the stone risers, each at least eighteen inches high; and Leigh was grateful to be the last in line to clamber up the stairs and enter the tiny room at the top of the tower.

Barely six feet square, the intimate little room

held only Una's melodeon against one thick wall and a tiny settee against the other. Dusky now, lit only by stray sun motes stealing in through the small arched windows, the room seemed to hold its breath, patiently waiting for these intruders to leave so that now, at the end of the day, it might return to its dreams of the lovely past.

Dow looked around him one last time and nodded silently to Mrs. Welling, who then preceded them out of the room to the outside landing, and on up the final spiral of the staircase to the very top of the tower. There, a view of such power and grandeur spread out before them that Leigh heard Dow gasp as if smitten by a blow to the heart.

A chill, muscular wind gusted up, and Leigh leaned against the waist-high stone wall for support. Una Jeffers stood here where we strangers stand now, Leigh thought. Surely she must've felt like a princess alone on the moon, who'd left wifehood and motherhood, as sweet as they were, safely down below her for a precious little space of time.

Then, into the pounding roar of the great waves below them came the toylike sound of a ringing telephone from the house.

"Oh, dear, I know who that is . . ." Mrs. Welling said, seeming unsure what to do next. "It's a terribly important call—I was told to expect it today. Would you mind . . . ?"

"Of course not," Dow said. "Do you think you can get there in time? Would you like me . . . ?"

But the docent was already scrambling awkwardly down the stone stairs, calling over her shoulder, "So sorry . . . be right back . . . it's about funding . . ." and she was soon a small figure running across the meadowy lawn and into the house.

A sudden cold gust of wind swirled around them and snapped Leigh's hair stingingly against her face. Shuddering, she dragged the light wool of her coat out of the wind's grasp and wrapped it closer around her tense body. She felt Dow's gaze on her, and after a moment's inner struggle she raised her eyes to meet his. There was a look there she'd never seen before in a man's eyes.

No sooner did she see Dow start toward her across the small stone floor than she found herself engulfed in his arms. His hand cupped the back of her head, pressing her against him in an almost desperate way—not as if he were sheltering her from the frigid wind, but as if she were the anchor that kept him from blowing away into the empty, impassive blue sky.

A little frightened, as much for him as for herself, Leigh said gently, "Dow, I think you really might be ill after all, let's go down."

"Oh, Leigh," he groaned, his breath warm and fragrant against her cheek. His lips, as cool as early morning, found hers and pressed against them as if to seek the warmth of life.

Leigh automatically stiffened in surprise, and she tried to move her mouth from beneath his, but after the briefest of efforts some stronger force held her there, made her want to give him what he sought.

When he did release her mouth, it was only to murmur against her neck, in an agonized whisper,

"Your hair is like honey and cream, your skin is so sunny . . . oh, California, I can't do without you."

At this admission that she'd affected him, that he perhaps cared for her, Leigh's heart expanded with joy and all thought of resisting him dissolved like sea foam against the sand. When his warm, firm lips again found hers, Leigh gave herself up to the ecstatic thrill that suffused her whole body, that burned and tingled through her like a bewitching fire.

Her heart pounding, her lips throbbing, Leigh felt Dow's hand push aside the lapel of her coat and come to rest on the soft mound of her breast. A sudden wave of desire for him slackened her body and she sank languidly against him, pressed close along the hard length of his muscular frame. Her breath came quick and shallow, in gasps, as she felt the undeniable proof that Dow wanted her. Without knowing it, she moaned as she returned his searching, probing kiss.

"You want me too, I know you do," Dow whispered fiercely into her wildly tangled hair. With hungry impatience he pulled open the buttons of her silk blouse and bent his dark head to kiss the trembling flesh of her flushed breast.

A great shudder rippled through Leigh, cutting through the warm, lovely languor she floated in, and brought her back to reality, back to the darkening light of the dying day, to the wetly cold wind that had never once ceased its driving motion, its eternal search for a place to rest.

Dow and Leigh pulled apart, both breathless, with

eyes shining and soft with desire, as they heard the hollow, faraway call of Mrs. Welling, as small as a doll far below them: "Yoo-hoo, up there . . . have you finished?"

A secret, intimate smile lifted the corners of Dow's mouth. He bent his handsome face once more to Leigh's lips, and his light kiss was one of promise and tenderness. "I don't know about you, California," he whispered, holding her gently, "but as for me, I've just barely begun."

Chapter Seven

The following day, Leigh was like a creature blessed by Dame Fortune, unable to do anything wrong. For the first time in her twenty-four years, at breakfast she made a perfect omelet. When she chose her clothes for work that morning, she suddenly saw a combination in her closet she'd never noticed before, a mix of colors and fabrics so inspired that she might have been dressed by Halston himself. And, most unbelievable of all, she sold the Stafford House, a truly grotesque adaptation of a Hansel-and-Gretel cottage which had languished deservedly on the market for nine months; and as if that weren't cause enough for celebration, she sold it to Mr. and Mrs. Grummidge, the banes of every realtor in Carmel for the last three years. All in all, a magical day.

Perhaps that's why, on Sunday morning, Leigh made the mistake of expecting that because yesterday was a triumph, so too would be today and all the tomorrows to come. It's a very human error to believe that one swallow does indeed a summer make.

Dow was expected at Illyria for tea that afternoon, and for the first time since meeting him, Leigh looked forward to his arrival with unadulterated pleasure. It wasn't that she thought Friday's happening was a commitment of any kind on the part of either herself or Dow—but it was a start, wasn't it? After all, he'd indicated that he cared for her, a little. Of course, Leigh realized that much of the attraction was merely physical at this stage (she blushed to recall just how physical it'd been). And she knew, from her humbling experience at age eighteen, that physical attraction didn't necessarily lead to eternal love. But on the other hand, wasn't physical attraction the most usual first step to real and lasting love?

Leigh smiled into the mirror with healthy self-mockery and said to herself, "Look at Tristan and Isolde, or Abelard and Heloise. Even Adam and Eve, for that matter."

As she took note of the sunny flush of high color on her cheeks and the soft shine in her eyes, Leigh had to admit that she was looking her best today. How nice it was that things had turned out so well, she thought comfortably. Gran had her charming new friend back, and Leigh . . . well, that remained to be seen. But how much better she felt today than she'd felt a week ago when she'd told Dow—so untruthfully—that she never wanted to see him again.

The drawing room of Illyria was freshly cleaned and brightly autumnal with crystal and brass bowls of dusty-pink and rosy-brown chrysanthemums placed strategically about on the polished tables. All the residents of the house were gathered and the tea cart stood by in readiness, laden with delectable cakes and sandwiches made by Annie Channing and Burt Cosgreve.

As Leigh entered the room, Dibbie gave her a knowing grin. "Well, well, don't you look spiffy! I haven't seen you wear that dress since Sam took you to that fancy garden party at Pebble Beach last summer."

Annie Channing cocked her head and said doubtfully, "I wonder if chiffon is quite suitable in the fall . . . ?"

"Oh, I think so, Annie, because of those muted golds and browns, you see," Gran said smoothly.

"Leigh would look beautiful in overalls and flannel," Burt said gallantly.

"Yes, what does it matter what she wears?" John agreed.

"For heaven's sake, what a fuss!" Leigh felt herself grow nervous with self-consciousness under this intense scrutiny from everyone in the room. "We're just having a guest for tea!"

The doorbell rang then, and John Channing stopped himself in mid-motion as he rose from his chair, as if remembering prior instructions, and gestured casually to Leigh. "Why don't you answer the door, dear."

Leigh's heart fluttered as she wondered what Dow's mood would be today, after last Friday's intimacy. And when she opened the door to him, her hopes wavered. The smile he gave her was reserved.

"Come in, won't you?" Leigh said, suddenly feeling as awkward and abashed as a young girl.

Each time she saw him lately, Leigh noticed that his dress, at least, was more relaxed. Today he wore a beautifully cut tan corduroy suit. His black-and-tan-striped shirt was worn without a tie, open at the neck, and Leigh's eyes were irresistibly drawn to the dark, silky hair curling near the tender base of his throat. He stepped into the foyer and closed the door behind him.

Because that remote, correct, eastern look was back on his face, Leigh was grateful that she'd reminded herself not to make too much of Friday's crack in his armor, to be cautious with her feelings. She turned to precede him down the short hall, but he took hold of her arm and turned her to face him. At his touch, Leigh's hopes flared. She looked up into his deeply searching gaze, thinking he was about to kiss her again. But he averted his eyes and said politely, "I'd like to thank you for being so . . . understanding the other day." A slight flush colored his firm jaw as he added, "I hope my behavior wasn't too offensive to you."

A pang stabbed through Leigh. He was apologizing for the very thing she'd pinned such hopes on! Was he trying to tell her that last Friday was just a momentary lapse brought on by his depression over his family problems and the sheer romantic aura of the little tower by the sea?

"Of course not," Leigh mumbled, and in awkward confusion she turned again to lead him to the sitting room, where Dow was awaited by her family like a visiting prince.

When he'd been seated in one of the regal chairs by the fireplace and served his tea by Annie, the small flurry he always caused in Leigh's loved ones gradually calmed and general conversation began.

"Now that you've been out here for a while, how are you liking California, Dow?" Burt asked.

Leigh held her breath for fear Dow'd plunge into a diatribe like the one he'd subjected the patrons of La Marmite to last week. Oh, how she hoped he'd give her no more reasons to dislike him. It was so painful to dislike him. But she needn't have worried.

"I've never denied that California has more natural beauty and wealth in a square foot than the rest of the country has in a square mile." Dow said generously. "And who could resist a temperature of fifty-five degrees in early December?"

Dibbie said with a teasing little smile, "Well, that's some improvement, I guess. But do you still think we're all mindless hedonists—I believe that was your word?"

Leigh caught her breath. Why was Dibbie throwing Dow's past rudeness in his face just when he showed signs of mellowing?

But he merely glanced at Leigh, then smiled dryly. "Touché, Dibbie. I'd have to be even more of a fool than I am to include this lovely family in such a stupid generalization." Then he paused, a shadow of anger briefly darkening his expression. "It's just that I know several sun-struck Peter Pans who were lured out here recently by the—you'll have to admit—the broad tolerance for social experiment." Dow looked around the room with an apologetic smile. "I hope you'll all forgive me for lumping all Californians in with a few lunatics."

Gran spoke for them all. "Don't give it another thought. First of all, we're used to the culture shock people go through when they first come out here. And second, it's true that California has more than its share of 'social experimenters.' But, as you say, we've learned to be tolerant. Why not? Some of the experiments have been brilliant successes, and as for the rest . . . well, we have so much else to be grateful for, we can well afford to be tolerant."

As the conversation moved on to other topics, Leigh mentally sighed with relief that the sore subject of California had been so gracefully compromised. As she sat back amid the flow of talk around her, Leigh's thoughts focused on her tentative new feelings for Dow Madigan. She warned herself to be cautious. She'd given up pretending that he wasn't a madly appealing man, admitting to herself what everyone else in the family had seen from the first. He wasn't an ordinary man in any way. He had spectacular looks, superior intelligence, a very fine background, and a charming manner. All that she granted.

But none of them knew him really well yet. He

was also often difficult, overbearing, and even rude—at least to Leigh. And most important of all, he was still involved with another woman. One needn't take only Minnie Wanamaker's second sight for evidence, either; there was also Pamela's evidence. What more could one require than the proof of a man courting a woman with expensive gifts?

Therefore, Leigh instructed herself, she must be careful not to lose control of her feelings for him, as she'd so nearly done last Friday. She shivered a little to remember how close she'd come, in the tower, to submitting utterly to his kiss and the touch of his hands.

"Are you chilly, dear?" Gran asked suddenly. "Burt, build a nice fire for us, there's a dear."

Leigh blinked as she came out of her own thoughts and saw that Gran was ordering people about like a film director setting up the next scene. "John, you get out the brandy and sherry, and Annie will count out the chips."

Trying to catch up, Leigh asked, "Are we going to play poker . . . now?" Privately she meant: Are they going to inflict one of their crazy games on a visitor?

"*You* are," Dibbie said meaningfully, "not me. I'm going up to my room to read that new novel about Hollywood by that New Jersey writer. I want to see how many mistakes he makes." Then, adopting a Tallulah Bankhead manner, she drawled, "Ta-ta, dahlings," and waving, left the room.

Nervously Leigh said to Dow, "If you'd rather not . . ." although she had no idea how she'd change

Gran's mind if Dow did say no, he'd rather not. Once Gran made up her mind about something, that was pretty much the end of it.

But Dow smiled pleasantly and replied, "No, I'd like to play. I've played for years, learned at my grandfather's knee."

And Leigh didn't doubt it, once they'd settled down into the first few hands. Different players had different styles, Leigh knew. For instance, Burt was a serious player, while John Channing often shattered into fits of gleeful giggles when he thought he had a winning hand. Annie affected a discombobulated air, although she was just as sharp a poker player as anyone else at the table. And by the end of the third hand, Leigh saw what Dow would be like in the boardroom and the executive suite. She could imagine how he would handle a negotiation meeting between labor and management or manipulate a stock takeover. His face became an impenetrable mask. When he spoke, which was seldom, his tone was cool and remote. He placed his bets precisely, with no dramatics or hesitations. Leigh could see that his control of his emotions and his keen mind would make him a formidable player in any of life's games.

At the close of the third hand the remaining cards were tossed in front of Leigh, the next dealer. Dow reached out with a single deft movement and gathered up the large pot he'd won.

"Blast," John Channing muttered, getting up to walk around his chair several times to change his luck. "I told you this was the unlucky chair," he hissed into Annie's ear.

Gran gave John a disapproving stare. "If you actually believe that nonsense, John, then it's very unkind of you to always try to get Annie to sit there, isn't it?"

Grumbling, John drummed his fingers on the table impatiently. As Leigh dealt out the cards for the next hand, she could see from beneath her eyelashes the repressed amusement on Dow's mouth, and she thought: If he thinks this is funny so far, just wait until he tries to cash in his winning chips for imaginary money.

The game was five-card draw, and for a few seconds there was a serious silence as each player studied his hand. Dow, on Leigh's left, opened by placing a blue chip in the middle of the table.

"My goodness," Annie breathed admiringly, "you must have quite good prospects to open so high."

Dow looked up from his cards and smiled briefly. "What are the stakes, by the way? I don't believe anyone mentioned them."

All eyes at the table swerved to Gran, and after a bare second's pause that lady cleared her throat and said, "Since you're unfamiliar with our game, Dow, I think we'll play for small stakes today. Quarters, dimes, and nickels, if that's all right with you."

Dow lowered his eyes to his cards again and said offhandedly, "Whatever you wish, Miss Parnell. But just for curiosity, what are your usual stakes?"

John spoke up with a cheery pride. "We play for substantial stakes, you can be sure of that."

"How substantial would that be?" Dow pressed gently.

Leigh was about to explain the whole silly farce to

Dow when she suddenly felt Gran's eyes boring into her and read the message in those eloquent eyes to keep her mouth shut.

Burt broke in with a note of finality in his tone. "Ten, five, and one, usually," he said.

Dow looked from one face to another, puzzled, then seemed to decide that to press for further elucidation would be in bad taste. Leigh too was puzzled. Why would they all hide the truth? Were they afraid Dow would think them fools to play poker only for fun?

As was her wont, Annie began to chatter throughout the betting and playing of the hand. The others, long used to it, ignored her. But now it was Leigh's turn to repress her amusement as she watched Dow try to hide his annoyance. Leigh could just imagine him telling himself: Now, remember, you're not playing with the big boys in the back room of a Las Vegas casino. This is a social occasion, a penny-ante game with a nest of flaky Californians.

Annie said brightly, "How are you coming in your search for a house, Dow? Has Leigh shown you anything you like?"

Dow favored Annie with a courteously patient smile while with one eye he peered at his hand of cards. "I've seen one house I like quite a lot. I'd like to see it once more before I make a decision." Then Dow turned to Leigh. "Will you set up an appointment for me to see the Wanamaker house tomorrow morning?"

Leigh had a dental appointment the next morning that she'd postponed several times, and fearing the dentist's wrath, didn't dare tamper with again. She acknowledged to herself that it was a great disappointment to miss spending even a part of a morning with Dow, but the businessperson in her prudently substituted Dibbie's services rather than postpone the house viewing to another hour or day. So it was agreed that Dibbie would accompany Dow to Minnie's tomorrow at ten o'clock.

John Channing won the next two hands, immediately restoring his good humor. As he shuffled the cards in his debonair, flamboyant way, Burt used the time to ask Dow if he'd been satisfied with Sam Nelson's services as an attorney.

"Sam has a very illustrious clientele in the area and we're all very proud to call him our friend," Burt said in his kind, generous way.

At just that moment, Leigh happened to look up from her cards at Dow, and she was startled to see what looked like guilt flicker over his face. Why should he react so strangely to such an innocent question?

Recovering himself quickly, Dow replied shortly, "I didn't meet with him professionally. There was no need to. The matter was taken care of by other means."

No one commented on this mysterious utterance, but a moment's silence prevailed until Annie once again stepped into the breach with some harmlessly irrelevant comment that dissipated the tension. But from that point on, Dow's concentration on the game deteriorated. Because of his strict control of himself, the signs were subtle—a perpetual frown where before there'd been a mask; an agitation in his body movements where he'd been calm and still before. When it got to the point where he had to be reminded that it was his turn to bet, Gran announced that they'd play once more around the table, to be fair, then they'd stop and figure the wins and losses.

A half-hour later when the chips were counted, it was found that John Channing was the big winner and Gran the big loser. When she told John she'd settle with him later, he winked conspiratorially and nodded. It was nearly seven o'clock by then, and obvious that their guest was distressed, so the Channings and Burt told Dow how much they'd enjoyed his visit and went upstairs to their respective apartments for a light Sunday supper.

When the others had gone, it seemed to Leigh that they'd taken all the afternoon's good feelings with them. It felt very much as if the curtain had just come down on a play and the actors had thrown off their roles and sunk into the dreariness of everyday life. Gran, as sensitive as she was, seemed not to feel it. She sat quietly by the fire as if waiting calmly for an expected event to take place.

Leigh remained at the card table, fidgeting as she racked her brain for something to say that would lighten the tense atmosphere and yet not be silly or flippant. She yearned for Annie's ingenuous, light touch. Dow stood at the end of the room, near Gran, with one arm leaning against the mantelpiece, staring down into the embers of the fire.

It was thus that Dibbie found them when she burst into the sitting room, calling out, "Is it safe to come in here? No one's gone bankrupt? No one's made a million?" She laughed cheerfully at her own joke until she sensed that something was awry in the room. "What's wrong? What's going on?" she asked.

"Hello, Dibbie." Dow turned from the fireplace. "Did you find many eastern mistakes in your Hollywood novel?"

Dibbie frowned uncertainly. "Why, no—not especially. I guess the writer did his homework."

Dow laughed strangely. "Good for him. I'm glad one easterner did his homework. I wish I'd done mine."

"Sit down, Dow," Gran said quietly, "and tell us what's bothering you. Things can hardly be as bad as you're making them seem."

"I hope you're a prophet, dear lady," Dow said, sitting down across from Gran and leaning forward with his elbows on his knees in a pose of worried thought. "There's a matter of some importance I must discuss with you. I should've discussed it before now, but . . . one thing and another have interfered. Now it can't wait any longer." Dow ran a nervous hand through the dark wing of hair that slanted over his forehead. "It's all so muddled that I hardly know where to begin."

Gran smiled encouragingly. "Why not start at the beginning?"

"But where is that?" Dow smiled ruefully. "I suppose I may as well begin with Sam Nelson, since that was brought up this afternoon," Dow said doubtfully. Then, in a more purposeful manner, he went on. "I came out here on a somewhat delicate mission. I thought I'd need a lawyer who knew people in the area. But as soon as I met you, Miss

Parnell, I no longer needed a lawyer—or certainly not one who had close ties to you and your family. That's why I never engaged Sam Nelson."

Dow looked up to Gran's listening face as if for assurance that she was following him so far. Dibbie and Leigh exchanged a baffled look, but Gran nodded and gestured for him to continue. "I told Leigh I'd come out here to find a house in the area because my company was opening a branch on the west coast. That was my primary purpose."

Confused, Leigh questioned, "I can understand that you'd need a lawyer for certain delicate aspects of opening a business branch, Dow, but I don't see what Sam's having close ties to our family has to do with it."

Dow glanced at Leigh and nodded. "I know you don't understand—that's why I'm trying to explain. My primary business purpose was to open the branch and look for a house. But my *personal* purpose was the delicate one and the one for which I needed a lawyer. The thing is, I came out to settle a debt. And since it's an inherited debt, I knew absolutely nothing about the circumstances surrounding it, past or present. So I didn't want to come barging into a situation like some bull in a china shop, you see. But one thing led to another before I could resolve the matter. And now I'm afraid I've put us all in an awkward position."

Dibbie spoke up. "What on earth are you talking about, Dow? You're not making a particle of sense. Do we know this person who owes you this money? Or . . . how can we help you? I mean, I'm not sure how we figure into this situation at all. This debt, for instance—is it a large one?"

Dow smiled wanly. "The debt is for a quarter of a million dollars."

The two young women gasped, and Dibbie exclaimed, "Good grief, no wonder you're upset! I'm certainly glad I'm not involved in a debt of such cosmic magnitude."

Dow laughed in a curt, unhappy manner. "As a matter of fact, I'm sorry to say you *are* involved."

"What!" both sisters cried in unison.

Dow nodded. "In a way, you are. The two parties to the debt are myself . . . and your grandmother."

Chapter Eight

"Impossible," Leigh said adamantly. "Absolutely impossible. You've made some ghastly mistake, Dow." Leigh pressed her lips together firmly and shook her head in total conviction that Dow was wrong. "I take care of all the business in this family, and there's no way Gran could owe anyone *fifty* dollars, much less two hundred and fifty thousand dollars, and I not know about it."

Dow started to reply, "I haven't made a mistake, Leigh, it's you—"

Dibbie interrupted in agitated agreement, "No, Leigh's right! I know she is—"

Then, holding her hand up for silence, Gran's authoritative voice cut through the confusion. "Stop that squabbling, all of you! Each of you is right. Dow's right that there's a debt between him and me, and you two are right that it isn't I who owe Dow money. It's Dow who owes me."

Dumbstruck, Dibbie and Leigh stared at Gran. "He owes *you?*" Dibbie squeaked. "A quarter of a million dollars? I don't believe it."

Leigh turned to Dow and said skeptically, "Gran's always been hopeless about money. She's never had that much money in her life at one time—so how could she have lent it to anyone?"

"I don't know!" Dow said impatiently. "I told you this is an inherited debt. I don't know anything about it. My grandfather owed it to Miss Parnell, and now it's a lien on his estate."

"It's a gambling debt," Gran said casually, as if that explained everything.

At this, both sisters again set up a great hue and cry in high-pitched voices, and Dow cut in this time, saying, "Please! If you'll just let me get a word in edgewise, maybe we can handle this like rational adults." He added sarcastically, "Do you think that's possible?"

When Dibbie and Leigh had grumbled into silence, Dow continued. "As I said, the debt is a lien on Grandfather's estate, but the funds can't be released until the estate is through probate. That will take at least a year, if not more. Ordinarily I'd have been in a position to pay the debt from my own resources in the meantime, but it so happens that my cash reserves are depleted right now. This new branch of the business has seriously eroded them, for one thing.

"So I took steps to raise the money by selling some

assets I'd recently acquired in San Francisco. I thought I'd have the money by last Sunday, when I invited you to lunch, Miss Parnell."

Here Dow broke off, frowning. When he continued, his tone was angry. "But last Friday I learned that the deal had fallen through. I went to the city early last week to try to straighten things out. But so far, it's still a mare's nest, and I just can't predict when I'll have the money."

Leigh, listening intently, noticed that Dow's explanation of the reason for his visit to San Francisco was different from the reason he'd mentioned to her, but, afraid to miss what he was saying, she put it out of her mind for the moment.

"So you see, I've waited to bring all this up until I could satisfy the debt. But since that doesn't seem possible in the near future, I think it's time we discussed, at least, some possible terms," Dow concluded, his manner one of embarrassment and discomfort.

There was a moment of quiet in the room, as if everyone needed a little time to adjust to this startling information. The expression on Gran's face was one of placid composure, but Dibbie seemed shaken and bewildered. Leigh couldn't quite put her finger on it, but something in Dow's manner, starting even at the poker table when Sam Nelson's name came up, bothered her; as if there was something more, something unspoken, behind Dow's tardiness in revealing his true reason for looking up Persia Parnell. But what it might be, Leigh had no idea.

Still, it was the possibility of future developments—of whatever nature—that caused Leigh to suggest, "Well, Dow, that's quite a bombshell you've just dropped on us. Maybe your initial idea of hiring a lawyer was a good one. Why don't I just speak to Sam about this anyway?"

Dow gave Leigh an irritated, impatient glance. "I think your grandmother and I can come to terms, Leigh. Between the two of us we ought to be able to work out a schedule of payments fair to us both."

"Of course," Leigh quickly agreed, anxious that Dow not think she mistrusted him. "It's just that I thought . . . well, as a businessman, you know that most negotiations go more smoothly with the help of a mediator. . . ."

"Don't you trust me, Leigh?" Dow asked with a sardonic smile.

"Of course I do," Leigh protested, flushing. But his very questioning of her motives germinated a seed of, not suspicion exactly, but uneasiness.

Gran, who throughout the last fraught moments might merely have been watching a mildly amusing movie, so disinterested did she seem, spoke up now. "It's late and we're all tired and overwrought. I think it's best if you run along now, Dow, and in a day or two when we're all in a calmer frame of mind, I'm sure we can work something out that'll be satisfactory to us all."

When Dibbie had shown Dow out, she returned to the sitting room to find her family as she'd left them—Leigh standing in the middle of the room, and Gran, calm and untroubled, in her chair by the fire.

"All right, Gran," Dibbie said lightly, "let's have it."

With wide-eyed innocence, Gran said, "My goodness, you girls are making such a fuss over nothing! I've held that note for fifty years now, and we've gotten along just fine. A little further delay isn't going to send us to the poorhouse."

"That isn't the point, Gran," Leigh said patiently.

"What is the point, then?" Gran asked reasonably, and went on in a nostalgic tone, "I remember that party as if it were yesterday. Everybody who was anybody was at that party at Max's house," she said, naming a famous movie producer of the thirties. "I had such a run of luck that night, I just couldn't lose. Although, to be honest"—she looked up with amusement in her eyes—"my sweet Dow was never a very astute poker player. I wouldn't be surprised if his poor grandson doesn't owe batches of money to people all over the country."

Dibbie narrowed her eyes at Gran. "This whole thing hasn't surprised you at all, has it, Gran? You must've suspected all along that Dow looked you up because of that debt."

Gran shrugged and replied primly, "It doesn't do to jump to conclusions, Deborah. Of course, I knew it was a possibility. But on the other hand, not necessarily. That note might've been lost years ago. Dow might never have known about it and might've looked me up just because he'd heard his grandfather talk about me from time to time."

Dibbie persisted, "Are you saying that if Dow hadn't known about the debt, you'd simply have let it go? Just let a quarter of a million dollars go uncollected?"

Gran replied vaguely, "Oh, who knows what I might have done. To tell you the truth, until he came to town, I'd forgotten all about that silly note."

Suddenly Leigh broke in to say musingly, "Does it strike anyone but me as odd that he waited so long to tell Gran he'd come about the debt?"

"He explained that . . . didn't he?" Dibbie said uncertainly.

Gran said staunchly, "He certainly couldn't have brought it up on Thanksgiving. That would've been very rude."

Leigh's mind went back to that moment when Dow'd walked into the sitting room and recognized Gran as Persia Parnell. Wasn't his shock a bit extreme? And why had he been so angry that Leigh'd forgotten to tell him Persia Parnell was her grandmother? But then, wanting to think only the best of him, Leigh could understand how unpleasant it would be to suddenly find yourself the guest of a stranger to whom you owed such a great debt. It would have been awkward for anyone, she thought fairly.

For the rest of the evening, Leigh tried not to think of the matter. The reasons Dow'd given for postponing his news made sense, more or less. And because Leigh wanted nothing to intrude on the delicate, hopeful new aspect of her relationship with

Dow, she resolved to put the whole subject of his debt to Gran out of her mind for the present.

When Dibbie came home about four the following afternoon she brought Leigh a cup of mint tea from Gran's kitchen, waking her sister from a groggy sleep. Leigh sat up in the dim room, her mouth still sore and feeling wrenched out of shape by the morning's long siege at the dentist.

Because of her befuddled state, it took Leigh some minutes to realize that Dibbie was behaving oddly. She sat on the edge of Leigh's bed, smoothing the pastel coverlet with nervous movements, drinking her tea in fast little gulps. Several times she seemed about to say something, only to fall silent.

"What's the matter with you?" Leigh asked finally.

"Nothing!" Dibbie replied. Then, as if buying time with a tempting tidbit, she added with brittle cheer, "I think Dow's going to buy Minnie's house."

Puzzled at her sister's manner, Leigh said, "That's wonderful. Minnie's dying to move to L.A. Was she there this morning? Does she know?"

Dibbie hesitated. "He didn't actually make an offer . . . so I didn't say anything to her."

Leigh wondered if Dibbie'd somehow botched the sale, or thought she had. She certainly wasn't behaving as if a successful business deal was nearing completion. "Could you get an inkling of what he plans to offer?" Leigh asked. "That house is worth nearly the asking price, you know."

Suddenly, unaccountably, Dibbie's round blue eyes filled with tears, and in a quavering voice she stammered, "Oh, Leigh . . . he said . . . he said the other . . . interested party . . . has to fly out to see the house first."

A cold feeling of impending disaster settled on Leigh, and in a small, waiting voice she replied, "Oh?"

Dibbie rushed her words now, hurrying to get the hurtful message over with, gulping out, "Yes, he said if . . . Elaine liked the house, they'd buy it. As tenants in common. He gave me the earnest money with the stipulation that if she didn't like the house, the deal was off."

Leigh repeated in a dead tone, "Elaine Stanley. His partner's daughter." Trying to smile and not succeeding very well, Leigh added, "Well, Dib, I can't pretend it comes as a surprise, can I? From the first day I met him, he never made any secret that there was a woman in his life."

"Leigh," Dibbie said in a timid, hesitant tone, "I guess it doesn't matter, but . . . she *could* be his partner's . . . wife, not his daughter."

Leigh stared at her sister—a girl whose soft, round baby face often made one forget how very astute she was. Of course. Dibbie was right. Elaine Stanley was a married woman with children. Hadn't Dow, that first day, asked about Carmel's school system? Wanted a big house with four bedrooms? And it also explained why he'd said—when he was obviously involved with a woman—that he didn't plan to marry. What was that bitter remark he'd made? "Your precious Carmel beach will go up in flames before *I* marry."

Then Leigh thought of the day he'd come into her

office looking so devastated, when against her better judgment she'd once again softened her heart toward him. But now that the veils of wishful thinking were ripped from her eyes, Leigh saw that no one could've looked so desperately unhappy merely over trouble with a "soon-to-be-ex-brother-in-law." Nor over a business deal that fell through— the reason he'd given Gran for his trip to the city that day.

No, it had to be a woman who'd made him so miserable. A *married* woman who'd temporarily rejected him, driving him to seek casual, short-term comfort in another woman's warm and willing body. *"Oh, California, I can't do without you,"* he'd said that day on the tower. Leigh shuddered with shame to think how cynically he'd used her.

Dibbie's soft little hand stole into Leigh's and pressed it. In a doleful tone she murmured, "Oh, Leigh, I'm so sorry . . . please try not to mind too much. . . ."

Shaking her head, Leigh replied, "But I don't, Dib. It doesn't matter a bit. You know I never liked him anyway."

But when her sister had left the room, Leigh put aside all show of pride and lay back against the crumpled pillow, feeling as empty and discarded as a burst balloon. Six years ago when she'd been a naive eighteen-year-old girl, jilted by a callow youth of twenty, she'd thought she'd tasted the absolute dregs of humiliation and misery. But now Leigh felt that pain to be what a paper cut was to an amputated limb. At eighteen she'd been abandoned by a frightened boy not yet ready for an adult commitment. Now she could understand his panic and be glad of its result, if not of his methods. But this time, Leigh thought, if she had any excuse at all, it was that in spite of numerous warnings she'd insisted on playing out of her league.

Huddled on her bed under the flowered comforter, the soreness in her mouth far overshadowed by the soreness in her heart, Leigh let a dark and fearful door in the back of her mind inch open. What if it weren't so much that she'd been playing out of her league as playing a different game from Dow entirely?

It was clear enough that Dow had used her—but for what? Would a man as handsome and sophisticated as Dow take the trouble to be so convincing, to put such passionate intensity into a casual game of love? Dealing harshly with herself, Leigh acknowledged that she was not an irresistible beauty who drove men mad with desire, nor a loose and frivolous party girl who gave men the impression that she wouldn't mind a harmless little fling. No, Leigh knew herself to be reserved, even a little rigid and repressed. She wasn't the sort of woman a man as smart as Dow would toy with just for the fun of it.

There had to be another reason, Leigh thought, and with a sense of growing anguish she finally faced what that reason must be. She thought again of Dow's shock when he met Gran unexpectedly, of how angry he'd been at Leigh's lapse of memory. He must've seen that day how sentimental Gran was about Dow's grandfather, and how taken she was with Dow himself. He couldn't have missed noticing that Gran so brazenly threw her granddaughter at his head, with that transparent ruse of lighting the way to his car that evening.

And remembering that, Leigh remembered also lying on this very bed that night, mooning like an idiot over his embrace, his exciting kiss, hearing again in her heart's memory his deep voice whispering the lovely lines from Jeffers' poem: "Some lucky day each November . . ."

That had been the first lie.

Leigh's mind searched meticulously through the once-bright fabric of days past for the dark flaws that proved Dow's perfidy. She saw a stranger, an alien, move into the world of Illyria, ingratiate himself with the family, flatter an old woman with honeyed words, court her with gifts and visits, subtly blackmail her by romancing her granddaughter—and all to one end.

Leigh felt sick inside as she imagined Dow's thought processes. How quickly he must've realized how easy it would be to escape his obligation entirely—if, indeed, he'd ever intended to fulfill it in the first place.

Like a melodramatic film, Leigh played back last night's scene when he'd finally revealed his debt to Gran, had strung her along with a pose of integrity, with promises of an intention to pay, with tales of heroic trips to the city to raise the money—with talk of "terms" and "payment schedules." All lies.

In one agitated motion Leigh sat up on the edge of her bed and pressed her fists into the hot skin of her aching forehead. What a fool she'd been—they'd all been. But now it was all clear, plain enough that even a closet romantic like Leigh Mallory finally saw the light, once and forever.

All the lovely meanings she'd thought she read in Dow Madigan's body that day at the tower; all those lovely things he'd seemed to say up there in the hungry, pushing wind and the clear blue sky so full of promise—she'd imagined it all. None of it was true. Like the pathetic fool she was, Leigh had thought it was the beginning of love, at last.

But it was only another lie.

Chapter Nine

The next morning found Dibbie and Leigh, dressed for work, arguing in the middle of the kitchen. "But, Leigh," Dibbie protested, "I'm not sure Minnie will *like* it if I take over the sale. She only let a small office like ours have the listing in the *first* place because she's so fond of *you*."

"Don't worry—Minnie's not dumb enough to throw away a sure sale." Leigh added sarcastically, "I think we can all rest assured that Elaine the fair, Elaine the lovable, Elaine the lily maid of New York City will like Minnie's beautiful house. Who wouldn't?"

"But, Leigh . . ." Dibbie pleaded.

"I never want to see that four-flusher again as long as I live, and that's that!"

Leigh swept out of the kitchen, Dibbie following her into the sitting room where Gran sat by the window reading *Variety* and sipping a cup of morning tea.

Dibbie said warningly, "Leigh, if you don't carry through on this deal, you may be throwing away thousands of dollars in commission."

"You have a point there," Leigh said coldly. "Since that's the only money Gran will ever see out of him, you'd better do a good job."

"What's this?" Gran asked sharply. "What are you girls squabbling about so early in the morning?"

"Oh, Leigh . . ." Dibbie said sadly. In spite of her sympathy for her sister's plight, Dibbie felt dismay at Leigh's vengeful attitude. "What a thing to say. You know the commission is paid by the seller, not the buyer."

Leigh laughed shortly. "Where have *you* been? The commission's paid out of escrow—the seller takes it from the buyer's funds."

Dibbie sighed, defeated. "All right. I'll take over for you."

"I said, what *is* this?" Gran said more sternly.

"You're not doing it for *me*. Do it for Minnie, if you want to. Or even for *him*—if you're dumb enough to still have anything to do with him. *I* don't care if he moves to Tierra del Fuego and buys a grass shack! So don't imagine you're doing it for *me*."

As a result of this ferocious and unfair attack, Dibbie burst into tears. Throwing *Variety* down in a great rustle of pages, Gran scolded, "Now, see what you've done. Shame on you, Leigh, making your sister cry! And talking that way about Dow—as if the poor man didn't have enough troubles already."

"Poor Dow?" Leigh repeated with scathing sarcasm. "That eastern shark? You listen to me, Gran. If you don't get someone just as sharp as he is to negotiate that debt for you, you're going to wait another fifty years before you see a cent of that money!"

Gran cried, horrified, "Why, Leigh, are you suggesting that . . ."

"That's exactly what I'm suggesting," Leigh replied sourly.

"Well, that's ridiculous," Gran protested. "What's gotten into you? No grandson of Dow Madigan's would ever welsh on a debt."

Dibbie added placatingly, "Leigh, he never suggested that he wouldn't pay Gran. He only said he needed to work out a payment schedule. Gran's right—he's not the sort of person who'd weasel out of a debt. Be fair, Leigh. . . ."

Leigh stood, as at bay, in the middle of the room, her fists clenched at her sides. "There you go again! Each and every one of you've been taken in by him from the very first. I tell you, he's not what he seems. You don't know him the way I do!"

Torn with emotion, frantic with hurt, Leigh whirled to run from the sitting room. There, standing at the doorway from the entry hall, stood a trembling John Channing and a frozen Dow Madigan.

Pale with shock, John stammered out, "The door was open . . . I was cutting back the fuchsias . . . I told him to go on in . . . outside, I couldn't hear, I didn't know . . . oh, I'm so sorry. . . ."

With a cry of anguish, Leigh ran awkwardly toward them, brushing past the tall, marble-stiff figure with eyes of burning blue, escaped Illyria through the still-open door to the lonely, loveless, but safer world outside.

During the next few hideous days the residents of Illyria all took sides about the Great Debt. Only Burt Cosgreve was willing to suspend judgment, admitting Leigh's suspicions might be valid. "I know his business is in trouble," he'd said. "It's possible he's looking for a way out of debt. Maybe bankruptcy. Only time will tell."

Annie and John, judging others only by their own integrity and sweet natures, had every confidence in Dow's intentions and were more than slightly miffed at Leigh for doubting him.

Gran, at the very heart of the matter, entirely refused to discuss it, much to the annoyance and frustration of all.

The tension in the house, then, had grown to such a suffocating pitch that it was with great relief that Leigh accepted an invitation to dinner on Thursday evening from Sam Nelson.

Leigh wore one of her favorite dresses, a light-weight black wool of austere and elegant cut. Its sleeves were long and close-fitting and its high neck was the perfect foil for a string of pearls or a gold chain. The gored skirt skimmed gracefully over the hips and flared discreetly at the hem. Because it was the kind of dress a woman could depend on to make her seem sophisticated and self-assured even when she felt anything but, Leigh thought it the perfect choice in her present state of mind.

But if she'd counted on Sam to take her mind off

her problems, she was disappointed. From the moment he picked her up at seven o'clock, Leigh saw that Sam might very well have had the same expectations of her, so worried and distracted did he seem.

Simpson's Restaurant, beloved of local Carmelites for thirty years, might've been the best restaurant in any middle to large city in the United States. The food was always fresh and superbly cooked, served in generous portions, and of unabashedly American cuisine. For a couple looking forward to warm companionship and an excellent dinner, Leigh thought, the comfortable, civilized, no-nonsense ambience of Simpson's was perfect.

While waiting for their table, Sam and Leigh had a drink in the Sandbar Lounge, a straightforward bar that Leigh always thought of as "masculine," with its mahogany paneling, dark leather seating, brass fittings, and yards of sparkling mirrors. Sam, never particularly talkative, seemed morose as well as quiet as he sipped at his vodka martini and folded a cocktail napkin into postage-stamp size.

"Would you like to talk about what's bothering you, Sam?" Leigh asked finally.

"Oh, it's Marianne," he muttered. Then, looking up at Leigh with a dark smile, he added, "I used to think divorce meant the *end* of a relationship. But we've had more trouble since the divorce than we ever had while we were married."

At Leigh's gentle prompting, Sam went on to tell her that Marianne was thinking of marrying again. Leigh knew that under the terms of Sam's divorce settlement, Marianne would lose her alimony if she married again. Anyone might think it would please Sam to be relieved of the burden of maintaining two households on one income, but Sam didn't seem happy at all.

In fact, Leigh often thought Sam was much more unhappy without Marianne than he'd ever been with her, and it was more than possible that her remarriage would be a much greater loss to him than any amount of money he paid her monthly.

"This man she's thinking of marrying," Sam went on dolefully, "lives in Chicago. He's a condominium developer. If she moves to the midwest, I'll be lucky if I see my kids twice a year. Whatever I gain in not paying alimony, I'll spend on plane tickets."

Just then Sam's name was called and they were shown to their table by the very correct young maître d'. Having eaten at Simpson's many times, Leigh gave the menu only a cursory glance. Her mind was on the unfairness of the situation in which Sam found himself.

Marianne was a strong, vibrant woman who'd been infected, in Leigh's opinion, by the seductive lures of these restless times. Even granting that no outsider really knew the inner truth of a marriage, Leigh had known Sam and Marianne long enough to feel that their divorce had been a tragic mistake. Marianne's publicly stated reason for leaving Sam had been a vaguely worded declaration that she wanted to find herself, be her own woman, be independent—and none of this could she do while married to Sam.

If Sam had been a rigidly traditional and authoritarian husband, if he'd been overbearing and dominating, Leigh would've been sympathetic to Marianne's plight. Or if, on the other hand, he'd trapped Marianne up on a pedestal and suffocated and weakened her with patronizing paternalism, Leigh would've *encouraged* her to leave. But, in fact, Sam was a dependable, loving family man, with his fair share of faults perhaps, but also more than his share of virtues.

It angered Leigh that now Sam was to lose not only the woman he'd loved in such good faith, and his family life, but now also his children as well. In a tone that revealed Leigh's general bad humor and bitterness lately, she said to Sam, "If he's a condominium developer in Chicago, he's undoubtedly got enough money to buy and sell you once a week. You're a lawyer—write up a new custody agreement. Make it a condition that if Marianne takes the children out of California she has to pay the costs of their visits to you. If you have to lose everything you care about, at least make those responsible pay the piper, for a change."

Sam looked at Leigh with mild alarm in his gentle blue eyes. "You're a real tiger these days."

"I've just been learning that nice guys finish last," she replied with a dry, brittle smile.

Leigh and Sam were nearly through dessert, an enormous piece of chocolate cake with fudge frosting, when the sounds of an altercation at the reservations desk caused them to look up.

With a sinking heart Leigh saw that Dow Madigan was at it again. He stood there in the small foyer, in plain sight of the dining room, arguing with the stiff-faced maître d' over something Leigh couldn't make out. His dress as well as his manner seemed to have reverted to eastern rigidity. He wore a midnight-black suit of impeccable cut, a blindingly white dress shirt, and a somber black-and-white-striped tie. His creamy fair skin was whiter still from indignation and his dark hair shone with highlights in the soft, dim overhead lights.

What a devil he is! Leigh thought, and at the same time was mortified at the way her treacherous emotions surged at the sight of him. But then Leigh noticed that behind Dow stood a woman so elegant and beautiful she might've stepped from the pages of *Vogue*. Her long glossy black hair moved like a heavy velvet drape against her shoulders as she turned her face away from the spectacle before her, as if to disassociate herself from it. Then, while Leigh watched frozen, she reached forward and plucked at Dow's suit sleeve with her fingertips, frowning slightly and gesturing that they should leave.

Dow inclined his head deferentially toward hers, said something Leigh couldn't hear, then, shrugging, turned his back on the indignant maître d'. Dow wrapped his arm protectively around the beautiful woman's shoulders, opened the door for her, and ushered her out into the damp night.

Moments later when Sam noticed that Leigh was desultorily pushing the moist crumbs of her half-eaten cake around on her plate, he signaled for the check and suggested they return to the Sandbar Lounge for a brandy. When they were once again in the dark, intimate room, this time seated at the banquette against the wall instead of the bar itself,

Sam asked Leigh, "Who was that beautiful woman with Dow Madigan?"

Leigh was surprised at the fresh pain it caused her to have to put into words what she'd silently suffered over for several days now—that the beautiful woman was Dow's woman, with whom he was buying, and planning to live in, Minnie Wanamaker's house.

Then, as long as the worst of it had been said, Leigh went on to tell Sam about the debt Dow owed Gran and Leigh's conviction that he'd never pay it.

"I've been meaning to consult you professionally about this," Leigh said, "but I've put it off . . . because, for one thing, I've been told to stay out of it, by *him*, in no uncertain terms, and by Gran—sort of by inference. She and the rest of them, all but Dibbie, still dote on him, and whenever I try to make them wake up and face reality, they give me this 'shame-on-you' look as if I were slandering Santa Claus."

"What makes you think Dow won't pay Jane?" Sam asked in his professionally objective tone.

Leigh began at the beginning then. She described Dow's shock on Thanksgiving when he'd walked into Illyria and seen that the woman he'd come to Carmel to find was none other than his hostess.

"Yes"—Sam nodded—"I noticed his reaction that day, but if I thought about it at all, I guess I just thought he recognized her as Persia Parnell, the silent-film star. Of course, I didn't know then he'd come here to seek her out."

Leigh went on to tell Sam what Dow had said to her that evening when Gran had forced her to walk to his car with him. "You wanted me to make a fool of myself by not recognizing her," he'd said. "You hoped I'd commit a *faux pas* so serious I'd never be able to live it down."

Leigh said intently, "Now, doesn't that sound as if he was planning to find an addled old movie star that he could manipulate—maybe charm into forgiving the debt?"

Sam rubbed his chin in thought. "Well, Leigh, anything's possible—but it certainly wouldn't hold up in court."

"Oh, I know that!" Leigh said with exasperation. "But if you put it all *together* . . . Look, do you remember how quiet he was when Gran started to talk about the depression? About the fortunes they made and lost during those years before and after?" Leigh asked Sam eagerly.

With an apologetic smile, Sam replied, "Not especially, Leigh. But what if he *was* quiet—what could he contribute about the depression? He wasn't even born then."

In a stubborn voice, Leigh went on. "All right, how about the way he's courted Gran since that day, and never until last Wednesday even *mentioned* the debt? Doesn't it seem strange to you that he'd socialize with Gran—with the whole family!—when he'd actually come to see her on a business matter?" Leigh finished triumphantly.

Sam twisted on the banquette, as if uncomfortable. "Leigh, dear, you and your whole family are my clients, aren't you? And how many times have I been to Illyria socially? What are you and I doing right this minute?"

Hot tears of frustration turned Leigh's golden-brown eyes amber. She'd expected Sam, one of the most sensible people she knew, to instantly grasp the sinister behavior of the sharp dealer from the East. But here he was being purposely obtuse!

In a resentful mutter Leigh said, "Well, you didn't see how avid he was last Wednesday to find out what our poker stakes are. That was the evening he finally brought up the debt. And you should've seen the act he put on," Leigh said sardonically, remembering the awful tensions and confusions of that scene. "It's all very well and good for you to be the objective lawyer, Sam, but *I know* he's been trying to find out what Gran's financial situation is. I think he came here expecting to find either a rich-as-Croesus old movie star who didn't need the money at all, or a poverty-stricken, senile old lady he could force to settle for a pittance of what she's entitled to."

"Leigh!" Sam laughingly protested. "What on earth's gotten into you? What's Dow done to make you see him in such a sordid light? I thought he was a pretty straight guy. A little stuffy, maybe, but certainly not the shady character you think he is. I mean, he's a reputable businessman! What possible excuse could he have for *not* paying the debt?"

Relieved to be able to offer Sam something objective to shore up her suspicions, Leigh replied, "Burt says Dow's business is in trouble. The company's stock value has been falling. And Dow even admitted that he didn't have the cash to pay Gran right now." Then Leigh added meaningfully, "He said he wanted to work out a payment schedule with her." She sat back then, satisfied that now Sam would see through this ruse of Dow's, as she did.

But it seemed that even this wasn't enough to satisfy Sam. Shaking his head doubtfully, Sam replied, "I'm sorry, dear, but I just can't see that your suspicions hold up. Unless there's some evidence you haven't told me, it all sounds perfectly on the up-and-up to me."

Disgruntled now, almost angry with Sam, Leigh shrugged to indicate the subject was closed. If she could've told Sam the rest of it—the intimate part of it—she was sure then he'd realize what a bounder Dow was. Those kisses, those seductive words and intimate caresses—that they'd been nothing but an attempt to manipulate Persia Parnell by romancing her granddaughter, that he'd trifled with Leigh's feelings while at the same time using her to find a house to live in with the woman he really loved. That was the missing evidence that would've made Sam see she was right about Dow Madigan. But all that was too humiliating for Leigh to dwell on, even in her private misery. She could never admit to Sam that Dow had played her for such a romantic, trusting fool.

On Friday afternoon Leigh drove her car into the entrance of Point Lobos, the carefully protected state reserve a few miles south of Carmel. It was a perfect winter day of restrained sunshine, brilliant blue skies, and the intense California light that rivals that of Greece. The only sounds to be heard were those of an occasional calling bird, her car's engine, and the crunch of tires over the thick, copper-colored carpet of pine needles on the narrow path that wound through the forest toward the sea. Never really crowded, the Point was virtually devoid of people on this winter weekday, as Leigh had known it would be.

Just moments ago she'd sat alone in her small, quiet office. Dibbie'd left that morning to spend the weekend with Ray Snelling in San Francisco. Business had slowed to a stop from a combination of the seasonal slump, tight money, and the current exhorbitant interest rates. Feeling as if the walls of her office were pressing in on her, Leigh had picked up the phone to tell Gran she was going to the Point and wouldn't be home until dinnertime.

Leigh felt silly to be heading for the rugged Point dressed in a filmy mint nylon shirtwaist dress under her camel's-hair coat, with high-heeled strapped sandals on her feet, but she couldn't have known that the impulse to escape the office and come here would seize her so forcibly.

The mysterious smell of the sea grew stronger as Leigh drove through the dim, cathedral-like atmosphere of the towering pine and eucalyptus forest. Spanish moss, hanging from the barren, sun-starved lower branches, drifted lazily in the breeze blowing in over the Pacific. With only the slightest effort of her imagination, Leigh could believe herself back in the simple, clean world of a thousand aeons ago.

Leaving the car in the parking area of Whaler's Cove, Leigh sank down on a grassy knoll tucked among lichen-covered boulders on the sandy beach. In minutes the ocean breeze and the primeval quiet soothed her jangled nerves while the vast blue sky canopied over the endless green ocean put her small human problems into perspective. She sat hugging her knees against the cool gusts, staring out to sea. Soon she fell into a healing, mindless state, noticing nothing but the graceful cormorants wheeling freely in their airy world above her head.

When a voice from above and behind her suddenly called out her name, an atavistic reflex of fear surged through Leigh, making her cry out and whirl around to see a tall, menacing figure looking down at her from the parking area a few yards away. Even as her terrified heart thundered in her breast, a part of her calmed to see no dangerous stranger, but Dow Madigan, unwelcome though he might be.

It flew through Leigh's now alert mind that she'd never seen him at a distance before. In spite of the intense clarity of the light that glinted off his dark wavy hair and illuminated his ivory-fair skin, she saw him as a Black Irish prince of old, unpredictable in his moods, ruthless in his passions, his imposing height silhouetted against the untamed landscape behind him—a man to be reckoned with.

Dow stalked toward Leigh with long, purposeful strides, and when he was near enough for her to see the hard challenge in his eyes, she began to tremble. "Go away from here and leave me alone!" she flung at him defiantly, stumbling backward, the sea behind her.

On he came; the shifting sands and boulders between them were nothing in the face of his determination to reach her. Backed up now against the sea, the frothy ripples of the spent waves wetting her ankles, Leigh cried a shrill warning, "If you come one step nearer, I'll scream."

Dow smiled derisively and came on, near enough

now for Leigh to hear his breath rasping in his chest. Leigh shrieked as Dow's arm shot out with the speed of a panther's leap and closed on her arm in a numbing grip. Laughing harshly, low in his throat, Dow said, "It's either talk to me or swim to Hawaii."

"Take your hands off me, let me go! I have nothing to say to you!" With the strength of outrage and alarm Leigh wrenched at her own arm, only to cry out at the hot flash of pain that stabbed through her shoulder.

Dow announced grimly, "The last thing I need is to hear any more from you. *I'm* going to talk—not you."

Ignoring her resistance, he pulled Leigh behind him like a rag doll, stumbling and nearly falling over the boulders on the shore to a level spot of beach covered with winter-green sea grass. "Now, you're going to listen to me," he said firmly, imprisoning both Leigh's arms so hard her fingers began to tingle. "I know it looked suspicious, my not mentioning my grandfather's debt to your—" he began.

Interrupting sharply, Leigh cried, "Gran told you I was out here, didn't she?" Then, lowering her voice to a passionate intensity, she went on, "Since you're on such intimate terms with her, tell *her* whatever you have to say. Work out with my grandmother whatever 'schedule' you can—but leave me out of it. I wash my hands of it. I've listened to enough from you to last me the rest of my life . . . you eastern Casanova! You've used me all you're going to."

Dow's face stiffened into a mask of implacable

rage, and a terrible glitter lit up his dark eyes. "Do you realize what you're saying?" he demanded.

Uncaring now, so blinded by hurt and rage, so liberated by the mournful truth that she had nothing more to lose, Leigh struck out at him verbally. "I know what I'm saying, all right, and I should have said it weeks ago. Ever since I met you I've known you were a rude, arrogant, eastern snob, and it shouldn't really have surprised me to see that you're also a devious shark—and a *womanizer* as well."

A second's deadly silence fell. Dow looked deep and long into Leigh's tear-filled eyes. Then, in a voice so dark and strange and icy that it sent a shudder up Leigh's spine, he answered, "I might as well be hanged for a sheep as a lamb, then." He pulled her to him with an angry yank that knocked the breath out of her and kissed her so savagely that she winced to feel his teeth bruise her lips. Leigh's struggle to free herself seemed to madden him further as his hands released her arms only to grasp her shoulders in a grip that immobilized her even further.

As his angry mouth roamed from her throbbing lips to her throat, as his cruel embrace crushed her further into the hardness of his body, Leigh became frantic to free herself. She was alone here with this man, without a soul for miles around. Even if she could get her breath to scream for help, there was no one to hear, and he knew that as well as she.

Realizing that she was possibly in real danger, Leigh began to struggle again, using her legs to put what distance she could between their bodies, using her feet to kick ineffectually against Dow's shins. He raised his head just long enough to look into Leigh's face, his expression strange and his eyes transmitting a message she couldn't read.

Desperate to escape now, Leigh made one last backward lunge on one spindly, high-heeled foot while kicking at Dow's legs with the other, and lost her footing, bringing herself down on the cushiony sea grass with a thud, Dow's heavy, rangy body on top of her.

Leigh moaned aloud and began to weep. With a strange, frightening smile, Dow took her limp arms and held them above her head with one hand while with the other hand he smoothed the wild honey-colored strands of hair from her forehead with an oddly gentle touch.

"Please let me up," Leigh pleaded. "I can't breathe."

Dow's only answer was to shift his weight slightly so that his upper torso was aside her body instead of above it. But as he lowered his head to kiss her lips, salty with tears, Leigh could feel his heart thudding against her ribs.

Again she struggled to throw him off, but her attempts only made him laugh low in his throat. In one deft, impatient movement he untied the belt of her camel car coat. Leigh felt his touch through the filmy dress as if she were naked as his warm, firm hand stroked her body from shoulder to thigh, then moved back to rest caressingly on her trembling breast. His full lips nuzzled against her throat, moving lightly down to kiss the warm flesh he'd so nearly exposed by his caress.

In spite of Leigh's fear of him, in spite of her

terrible vulnerability out here under the Olympian sky, she thought she felt a change in his touch, a gentleness overtake the anger of those first harsh kisses.

Perhaps it was a reassurance that he wouldn't hurt her after all, or perhaps it was only resignation that she could do little to stop him, whatever his intentions, but Leigh felt her body slacken and yearn toward him. She submitted to the lassitude that filled her and weakened her will, and to the coursing tingle of the blood in her veins that cried out to yield to his demands.

As Dow released Leigh's arms from above her head, she breathed a great, shuddering sigh and relaxed against the soft grass beneath her, giving herself up to the incredible pleasure of Dow's mouth moving like a butterfly over her closed eyes, her forehead, the corners of her mouth, and coming to rest in the hollow of her throat.

When she felt his warmth retreat, she opened her eyes to see Dow poised above her, peering down into her face with an enigmatic question in his dark eyes. He seemed about to speak. Leigh waited breathlessly, hoping against hope that the change she'd thought she felt in his touch was true. Maybe she'd been wrong, too hasty. Her heart cried out silently for Dow to explain now—to make everything all right.

His slow, sensual smile sent flutters of delight through her as she looked up into his strong, handsome face. Dow leaned down to kiss her lightly on the tip of her nose, and then in a lazy, drawling tone he said, "I'm glad you stopped struggling,

California. It's not fitting for a native of the Feel Good State to let a few lofty morals get in the way of more important matters—like lovemaking."

An explosion of shock burst from within Leigh, and as she cried out in protest, her body reacted in tandem with her assaulted emotions. With a vigor born of rage, Leigh struck Dow a hard, sweeping blow with the heel of her hand. When he fell back, covering his jaw protectively, Leigh scrambled to her feet and ran, falling and stumbling over the boulders and sand, toward her car some fifty feet away.

"Wait! It was just a joke!" Dow called after her urgently. "I didn't mean for you to take it like that!"

But Leigh kept running, turning every few steps to make sure Dow wasn't pursuing her. When she reached her car, she turned one last time to see him sprawled on the sand like a half-drowned man dragging himself to the safety of the shore.

If she hadn't known him incapable of it, Leigh might have thought the expression on his face was one of abject misery. But knowing him as she did, it could only be embarrassment that his precious masculine attentions had been spurned once again. Well, if that's what it was, Leigh thought bitterly, let him go back to the warm and waiting arms of Elaine Stanley for reassurance. Once, not so long ago, Leigh had given him female comfort in Elaine's absence—now let her return the favor.

Chapter Ten

"Hand me that last string of lights, Dibbie, there on the piano, will you, please?" Leigh asked from atop the small stepladder where she perched, putting the finishing touches on the tall, fragrant Christmas tree in Illyria's sitting room. Leigh had put last week's debacle at Point Lobos firmly out of her mind and picked up her ordinary, everyday life where she'd left it that day before Thanksgiving when she'd had the misfortune to meet Dow Madigan.

She couldn't help but see curious glances and overhear wisps of conversations from time to time among the residents of the house about the still-unsettled Great Debt, but she resolutely ignored them and resisted any attempt to draw her in. Instead she fixed her energies on the coming holiday and urged and prodded everyone in the house to do the same.

Dibbie sat on the piano bench, idly picking out the tune to "Away in a Manger" with one finger. "I feel I haven't seen you for ages, Leigh. Not to talk to, anyway. I don't think you've been in the office for two hours all week."

"Well, business has been slow. . . ." Leigh said evasively. "Hand me that star now, and the tree will be finished."

Dibbie handed up the shabby but well-loved gilt star that had crowned their Christmas trees since they were babies. Fixing it in place, Leigh climbed down and stood regarding the tree critically. In a wistful tone she said, "Dib, do you remember the Christmas when Dad was stationed in Hawaii, before we came to live with Gran?"

Dibbie nodded. "Mother decorated the tree entirely in orchids that year."

Leigh sighed. "I wish we could all be together this year. It's been so long since Mother and Dad have spent Christmas with us."

Dibbie gazed at her sister's pensive face, knowing the true source of her nostalgia and wishing she could do something to ease her sister's sadness. "Well, at least all the rest of us are here," she comforted. "We'll have a good Christmas anyway." Then with a teasing little smile she tempted, "I've bought you a super present."

As if coming back to the present, Leigh turned to look at her sister for a long moment, her shadowed face lighting with a warm smile of gratitude. "When you have the best baby sister in the whole world, you don't need Christmas presents." And for that brief moment it was a relief for Leigh to feel the true spirit of Christmas fill up the cold void in her empty heart.

The following Tuesday, Leigh, along with several hundreds of her fellow Carmelites, made her daily visit to the post office to fetch the family's mail. This daily ritual was a tradition begun in the early days of the village. When the artist settlers were so few and so widely spaced, tucked away in the hilly forests, perched on the sea cliffs miles apart, a letter carrier would have been a laughable indulgence. Later, when the population grew enough to support such a service, the desire for privacy had become sacrosanct. No one wanted to give up the English practice of naming each house individually for the rigid, unimaginative American system of house numbers. So it was that the practice of coming to the post office daily developed into a cherished ritual which the Carmelites saw as an opportunity to keep in touch with friends and acquaintances via daily or weekly short chats in the lobby. The tourists, transients, and newcomers to town, however, saw it as an exasperating burden as they stood for weary hours on end in front of the general-delivery window waiting for their mail.

Leigh made her way through the chatting twosomes and threesomes in the lobby and along the halls, passing bank after bank of ornately decorated brass post-office boxes. She waved and smiled here, stopped for a brief word there, and called hello a dozen times on her way to Illyria's box. The always friendly mood of the crowd seemed even more intimate today, as it often did on days such as this when the chill fog that swathed the town contrasted so unpleasantly with the warmth and light of the marble-and-mahogany lobby.

Leigh retrieved a satisfying handful of Christmas cards, from the look of them, and made her way back down the hall. Just as she neared the door, her heart skipped a beat to see Dow Madigan enter the building. He was alone. In a second's glance, Leigh took in the high contrast between his fair skin and the black cashmere overcoat he wore. His cheeks were a bit ruddy from the nip in the air, and the damp had coaxed his dark wavy hair into loose ringlets that Leigh knew, in a flash of intuition, he must heartily loathe.

Leigh shrank against the wall and stopped breathing. But he saw her. Blue eyes locked onto golden brown and held for a quivering moment. But then the gleam died like a blue light extinguished in a deep cave, and Dow's eyes slid away from Leigh's as if they were utter, total strangers. Dow made his way to the end of the long general-delivery line, clasped his hands behind his back with his feet spread wide, like a soldier at parade rest, and lifted his head to ponder the ceiling of the post office.

Leigh let out her breath with a small gust and left the building. In seconds after the door closed, the white mist surrounded her, separating her from the source of warmth and light. After a few hesitant footsteps down the path she knew so well, Leigh felt a soft, cool moisture bathe her flaming cheeks and sting her eyes. It was the fog again, of course.

When Leigh reached her little office, the gentle tinkling of the doorbell and the warm glow of the pine-paneled walls had never seemed so welcoming. As she hung up her trench coat on the peg by the door, Dibbie was just ending a telephone conversation.

"That was Minnie," Dibbie said, amused. "She called with a progress report on Dow's aura. She says it's now changed from greenish-yellow to yellowish-brown. Must look horrible."

Leigh forced a weak smile.

"She's still stewing about the sale," Dibbie continued. "I think she's afraid *he'll* haunt the *house* —but on the other hand, she knows how unusual it is to find a buyer willing to pay the full asking price."

Leigh shrugged. "Yes, money talks."

"The title company delivered the preliminary report. All in order."

"Good," Leigh replied indifferently.

"Termite report came in yesterday. All clear."

Leigh made no reply, hoping Dibbie would shut up about the Wanamaker sale. Leigh had tried to make it clear to her sister that she wanted nothing more to do with it, but apparently to no avail.

"The lender's appraisal was right on the nose, so I guess we're going to have an easy sale with no hitches."

Leigh smiled sourly. "Unless Mr. Madigan can't qualify for his loan."

"Oh, come on, Leigh. Whatever else he may be, he's certainly solvent enough to qualify for a loan to buy a house."

"If he's so solvent," Leigh said flatly, "then why doesn't he pay his debts?"

Dibbie sighed and rose from her desk. "If it's all right with you, I think I'll go out for a bite to eat."

But as she reached the door, it opened inward and Leigh looked up at the tinkle of the bell to see three women clogging the doorway. Dibbie stepped back into the office; then their friend Pamela entered, followed by a stranger: a tall, very beautiful young woman. Leigh's heart leaped in panic as if she were some small, weak creature trapped in a corner by a sleek and hungry cat.

Elaine Stanley wore an elegantly casual tweed suit in beige and black. Her glossy dark hair was coiled in a chic chignon at the back of her well-shaped head and topped with a smart fedora-style beige felt hat. Now that Leigh saw her at such close quarters, an objective part of her mind recorded the other woman's extraordinary beauty. Elaine's face had the sleek lines of an Egyptian statue, and the expression in her eyes was open and friendly. With a feeling of unhappy confusion, Leigh knew that under other circumstances she'd probably like Elaine Stanley very much.

Smiling in her easy, confident manner, Pamela said, "Dibbie, I know you and Elaine have met, but I wanted her to meet Leigh. This is Elaine Stanley, Leigh—you remember a while ago I mentioned I'd sent her some clothes from the shop?"

In a dry, rusty voice, Leigh croaked, "Yes, of course."

"Well, as you know, she's moving to Carmel, and she came in today to exchange a few things that didn't quite fit, and we got to talking, and she's such a terrific lady, I decided to take her under my wing and introduce her to my best buddy!" Pamela rattled on with breezy joyousness.

Leigh's stomach went cold at her friend's betrayal. *How could Pamela do this to me,* she thought. While Leigh sat speechless, Dibbie leaped into the breach, offered chairs to the visitors, and fussed at the little hot plate where instant coffee was always at the ready. Elaine Stanley seemed not to notice anything amiss as she eased into pleasant social chatter in her quiet, well-modulated voice.

"I know I'm going to love living here," she said warmly. She spoke of the village's charm, its beauty, the wonderful shopping, the friendly people.

When the conversation touched on Minnie's house, Leigh felt a twang of pain as if a raw nerve had been touched, to think of the two of them living there together.

"Miss Wanamaker is a delight, isn't she?" Elaine asked, looking around her with a smile. "I don't think she likes Dow much," she added confidentially, "but then, he's been in such a foul mood lately, I can hardly blame her."

Leigh's heart squeezed painfully to hear his name in this woman's mouth, to recognize the easy familiarity with which she referred to him, to know that he belonged to her.

Pamela glanced briefly at Leigh, then said brightly, "Elaine, tell Leigh how you happened to decide to move to California. It's such a funny story—at least, the way you tell it's funny."

Elaine dismissed the compliment modestly. "No, I guess it really is funny now. Although at the time it certainly wasn't!" And then, in a humorously acerbic and wry manner she related the story of how her marriage of nine years had suddenly come to an end. Her husband, always a restless and volatile man, came home one evening a few months ago and announced that he'd resigned his position that day, that he wanted a divorce, and that he intended to move to California.

"It seems that for years he's cherished the idea that he has in him the makings of a great actor. And maybe he does." Elaine smiled wryly. "For nine years he played the part of a reasonably contented husband well enough to fool me."

As Leigh listened, sympathetic in spite of herself to hear of yet another blasted marriage, she was also shocked that Elaine would speak of such intimate matters to complete strangers, that she could joke about such a painful subject. How crass these easterners were! she thought. But then, Elaine would need to be crass to live with such a bulldozer of a man as Dow Madigan.

Dibbie murmured something sympathetic, and Pamela chuckled. "If you think that's bad, wait till you hear the rest of it. Go on, Elaine, tell the rest of it," she urged.

"Well, I took him at his word. There was no reason not to," Elaine continued. "I can empathize with a frustrated ambition. I have some of my own. Who doesn't, after all? But it turned out that he didn't intend to 'find himself' without a little company along the way. He'd been having an affair with the woman my brother had been seeing for over a year." Here Elaine's manner grew more subdued, and a slight frown shadowed her lovely face. "I never thought she was right for my brother, but he was very serious about her. It hit him awfully hard. I know he's glad now that it happened, although he's still smarting from the humiliation of it." Elaine looked up and smiled knowingly at the other women in the room. "You know how men are—they have such fragile egos."

It turned out that Elaine's brother's lady friend also felt a great need to find herself in Hollywood, so the two of them shook the dust of the east from their heels and moved to California.

"Then, the more I thought about it," Elaine continued, "the more I realized that inside the proper civic- and social-minded New York matron I'd become, there was a lazy, self-indulgent beachcomber crying to get out." Elaine laughed heartily, throwing her head back to expose a lovely throat and perfect teeth, and Dibbie and Pamela laughed with her.

Leigh sat like a stone, paralyzed by a welter of emotions warring within her. She was drawn to Elaine, and she hated her. She was glad Elaine had found happiness so soon after the breakup of her marriage, and she was desolate that she'd found it with Dow. She admired Elaine's spirit and courage, but she disapproved of her obvious intention to live unmarried with a man.

Pamela broke into Leigh's distressed thoughts. "Go on, Elaine," she prompted, "finish the story."

"There's not much left, really. The upshot of it all was that I thought, well, if *they* can move to California to find their true inner selves, why can't my brother and I? He was opening a branch of his business out here anyway, so I said to him, 'Dow, go out there and buy us the most beauiful house you can find!' And that's what he did, and here we are. The End," she finished merrily.

Leigh felt every drop of blood drain from her face as a great flood of shock washed over her. Had she understood correctly? But she must have, because Dibbie too seemed shocked, asking incredulously, "Dow Madigan is your brother?"

Elaine nodded, smiling quizzically.

Then Leigh asked, "And your husband—is he . . . was he Dow's business partner?"

"Yes, that's right. But for several months now they've been dissolving the partnership and the assets."

Leigh understood now that when Dow told her he'd gone to the city on family matters, and later told Gran he'd gone on business, he'd been telling the truth to both of them.

Pamela's face was alight with glee as she looked from one sister's face to the other. Social tact kept her from speaking candidly, but Leigh could see that her softhearted friend thought she'd brought the news that would fix everything that'd gone awry between Leigh and the handsome stranger from the east.

Of course, it fixed nothing. Later that afternoon, when Leigh and Dibbie drove home together, Dibbie said tearfully, "Oh, Leigh, if only you'd known from the beginning that Elaine was his sister!"

In a resigned tone Leigh replied, "It wouldn't have mattered. There's much more to it than that."

She thought of the instant antagonism between herself and Dow the day they met, his arrogant rudeness, and not least of all, his evasive behavior concerning his debt to Gran.

And yet, that evening alone in her apartment, Leigh brooded on the subject. If, at the very beginning, she'd known Dow wasn't involved with another woman, would she have given her admitted attraction to him a chance to develop? Mightn't she then have become enough involved with him so that when the debt came to light she'd have had more confidence in his character, fewer suspicions of his motives?

Leigh still didn't know that Dow's intentions toward Gran were honorable, but now she felt more inclined to at least suspend judgment. A man who cared for his own family enough to put his personal life at his sister's disposal was not likely to be a man who set out to cheat an old woman.

And as for his insulting and rude attitude toward California—well, Leigh could understand that now, too. She remembered that for a while after she'd been jilted six years ago, she'd scorned and reviled all commune living and—it was hard to believe now—had even bad-mouthed lovely, misty, green Oregon. Nor, during those first few months when her wounds were fresh, had she been very kind to any men who crossed her path.

Then a wild and agitating thought crept into Leigh's mind. She rose from the bed where she'd collapsed in misery an hour ago and began to pace the boundaries of the room. Should she pick up the phone right now and call Dow? She could beg his forgiveness . . . No, she'd keep it light. She'd laugh and tell him she'd just met his sister, and then . . . No, first she'd apologize for calling him all those names, for doubting him . . . But no, until she knew the outcome of Gran's debt, it hardly made sense to apologize for doubting him.

No, no, it was all too late. Too late to be young and impulsive, to take a chance and risk rejection. All the soaring hope drifted away and the poisonous cloud of doubts and confusion settled in Leigh's mind once again.

She sank back down on the bed and buried her face in the pillow, too desolate and frozen even to cry. As long as she lived, she'd never forget that look in Dow's eyes earlier today at the post office. Nothing would ever make a proud man like him forgive her for what she'd said to him, what she'd believed of him.

Gran warned me, Leigh thought miserably, but even that came too late. In her mind's eye she saw her own heart as a shabby, battered strongbox, the key lost, the lock rusted shut. Dow had come along and forced it open. But inside he'd found, not a treasure, nothing of value at all. No generosity, no tolerance, no trust—all components of love. Discarding the useless box, he'd turned his back on it, leaving it there to rust into dust, gaping open now, but empty forever.

Chapter Eleven

The following evening found five of the residents of Illyria huddled in tense anticipation around Gran's kitchen table. Not since the winter of the Asian flu, when everyone in the house but Gran had lain weak and miserable on a sickbed, had a Wednesday evening at Illyria passed without a poker game.

"How much longer do you think they'll be?" John Channing fretted. "You'd think they were working out the details of a Marshall Plan in there."

Annie let go of her knitting briefly to pat her husband's hand. "Just be patient, dear. Jane and Dow will soon work it out, and then we'll all have a lovely drink of sherry together."

Dibbie sighed gustily. "I can think of fourteen million places, *minimum*, where I'd rather be to-night."

Leigh smiled in commiseration. Once again, Gran

had pulled rank on them all, insinuating that it was their family duty to lend moral support while she and Dow negotiated the Great Debt. "When it's settled, I don't want to have to search all over the house for you," she'd said. So here they sat, for nearly an hour now, stewing in the kitchen, dying of curiosity. In an attempt to dress for the serious nature of the occasion, Leigh had tied her hair back with a brown chiffon scarf and worn a tailored cotton blouse in a crisp brown-and-white geometric pattern to go with her best-fitting, most expensive dark brown wool slacks, But by now anxiety had moistened her skin enough to coax short wisps of hair to curl around her face, and she felt as if she'd spent a night's sleep in her once-immaculate clothes.

"This meeting certainly came out of the blue," Burt said thoughtfully, puffing fragrant blue pipe smoke into the air. "At least, *I* didn't know it was in the offing. Did any of you?"

There was a general negative murmur, and Leigh said to Dibbie, sotto voce, "Did you tell her about Elaine?"

"No, but that doesn't mean she didn't hear it on her grapevine."

Leigh nodded. She felt certain that somehow Gran's sudden decision, announced at four o'clock this afternoon, to settle the situation tonight had something to do with the new development that Elaine Stanley was not Dow's lover, but his sister. No one had ever learned to anticipate Jane Campbell's subtle and brilliantly intuitive thinking processes, but Leigh, for one, had certainly learned to recognize the signs and results.

When the cuckoo clock Leigh's mother had sent from Germany clucked out the hour of eight, John Channing jumped up from his chair and cried, "I can't stand just sitting around like this! I'm going to make some popcorn."

But no sooner had John begun to rattle pots and slam cupboard doors than the others heard Gran's footsteps approaching from the hall. When she entered the kitchen, they all stared hard at her face, trying to read on it the results of her hour with Dow. But she'd not been a great actress for nothing.

Obviously it wasn't time for the big scene to be played, for her face was as unreadable as her voice as she asked them all to join Dow in the sitting room while she had a short word with Leigh. "Burt, please serve everyone a glass of sherry. I'm sure we can all use a little something to relax us."

When the others had filed out of the kitchen like awed children on their best behavior, Gran sat down at the table across from Leigh. She must've looked as haggard and tense as she'd felt these last few days, for Gran's brown eyes were warm with concern as she took both Leigh's cold hands in her own.

"This will be over soon, dear. I know how difficult it's been for you this past month."

Feeling she deserved censure more than sympathy, Leigh shook her head weakly in denial. But in her raw and wounded state, Gran's loving words were too much to bear, and to Leigh's dismay her lower lip began to tremble and two hot, fat tears spilled from her eyes and rolled down her cheeks.

Ignoring the tears, as if she feared to stop their flow, Gran began to talk in a calm, unhurried way, as if there was all the time in the world for a nice long chat. "Leigh, you know how dear both you and your sister are to me, don't you? And that I want only the best for your futures?"

"Of course I do, Gran; we both do," Leigh replied, both touched and a bit alarmed by Gran's portentous remark.

"And you certainly must know that I have every confidence in your intelligence, judgment, and acumen. After all, I've given you my power of attorney, I've put my financial affairs under your management, and I've named you executrix of my will. So you must believe that I trust you."

Really worried now, Leigh said, "I do believe it." Then she made a small grimace and smiled shakily. "Although, lately I feel I shouldn't be trusted to change a TV channel, I've been so stupid and made such a botch of things."

"I thought you might be feeling that way," Gran said knowingly. "But let's just say you've made mistakes. It's only stupid not to *learn* from mistakes. This evening, Leigh, I'm giving you a chance to rectify those mistakes."

Leigh picked a paper napkin from the holder on the table and dabbed at her eyes, then blew her nose. Smiling skeptically at Gran, she said, "What do you have in mind?"

"First, I want you to know this: when Dow settles his debt—I say when, Leigh, not if—the benefit will come to you." Holding up her hand to forestall Leigh's immediate protestations, Gran went on. "There's an equal benefit in my estate for Dibbie. I've thought this all out and it's perfectly fair. Even a scrupulous person like you would admit it, if you had the time to go over it in detail. However, there's no time for that now. I want your agreement that you'll accept the situation as I've presented it." Then Gran repeated her own words, giving them a solemn intensity. "The benefit from Dow's debt will be solely and exclusively yours, to do with as you see fit. Will you accept the situation—for you have no choice but to accept the benefit, if I choose to give it."

Leigh shrugged, confused and even a bit suspicious. Gran didn't have an ordinary mind, and God only knew what consequences might follow from her proposal. Still, because Leigh *was* so bewildered, she couldn't think what *else* to do but agree.

"Yes, all right, I agree. But I don't know what I've agreed to, really."

Gran sat back in her chair, beaming with triumph. "Excellent. Now, there's just one more thing, and then we'll join the others."

Oh, oh, Leigh thought warily, here comes the catch.

"I want you to promise that from the time we walk into the sitting room you'll do exactly what I tell you. And that you'll neither do nor say anything else."

Leigh sighed gustily, scrabbling in her mind for a proper response to this alarming request. It wasn't that Gran was foolish or naive. Leigh didn't think she'd be asked to do anything . . . well, dangerous or illegal. But anything to do with Dow Madigan now made her nervous and jumpy. And it wasn't in Leigh's nature to so easily give over control of herself to another. She stared into Gran's waiting eyes, trying to fathom some meaning in her mysterious request.

Gran, seeing Leigh's reluctance, said firmly, "Leigh, I can't go into any details. You'll understand it all later. For now, I must ask you to give me a simple yes or no. And, Leigh," she almost pleaded, "if you love me, you'll give me your promise on nothing but sheer, blind faith."

Powerless to deny her beloved grandmother in even small things, it seemed churlish to deny her now, when Leigh's agreement was obviously so important to her. And besides, there was no way she could refuse such a naked appeal to her love. If her agreement was presented as a proof of her love, of course she must give it, come what may.

Leigh took a deep breath; then, plunging into the unfamiliar world of blind faith and selfless love, she gave her agreement with a firm nod.

With a smile of gratification on her soft old face, Gran put her arm around Leigh's shoulder and led her out of the kitchen, saying, "I knew you had it in you, child."

As Leigh and Gran entered the sitting room, a hush fell over the occupants and all faces turned toward them expectantly. In the flash of a second, Leigh suddenly had a dim understanding of the lure of the stage. Her eyes went first to Dow, flanked on the sofa by the Channings; then, finding no welcome in his hard stare, she looked away. But not before her mind, like a camera, recorded every detail of his dress and manner. Because his clothes were so casual, Leigh surmised that Dow too had been given very little warning of tonight's meeting.

He wore a pair of authentic jeans, not yet faded by long hard wear, but properly tight across his flat stomach, hugging his long, muscular legs. His tan shirt might have come from a military-surplus store, so rugged and utilitarian it was, but the rich leather ankle boots he wore looked handmade. Never had he looked so "California," but it contrasted oddly with the shadows of fatigue in his dark eyes and the tense lines on his too-pale face.

In a natural, unselfconscious way Gran took a stance in the center of the room. Leigh hovered awkwardly just behind her and sought out Dibbie's round eyes for moral support. When Gran had everyone's attention—a matter of split seconds—she began to speak.

"Dow and I have agreed on the following terms, which he's asked me to relate to you. The payment of the debt is to be decided on the play of a single hand of poker."

A ripple of surprise skittered around the room, and Leigh's business head whirled with shock at this all-too-characteristic example of Gran's daredevil nature.

"If I win the hand, Dow will pay me half a million dollars in cash no later than the end of the first week of January. If I lose, Dow will owe me nothing and I'll sign off the note here and now, in the presence of each of you in this room. The cards will be cut, and high card will deal. Dealer chooses the game from either five-card stud or five-card draw."

Here Gran broke off to smile at John Channing. "We decided there'd be no Spit in the Ocean, or One-Eyed Jacks Wild, John."

John blushed with pleasure to be singled out with affectionate teasing by the grand lady he so admired. Then, like the great actress she was, in complete charge of her role, Gran dropped the amused expression from her face like an empty gum wrapper and assumed her previous serious tone. "Have I presented the terms correctly so far, Dow?"

Dow nodded briefly, his eyes glancing at Leigh. Gran continued. "The final term we agreed on is that Leigh will play my hand for me."

A little wave of gasps and cries and murmurs rolled through the room, and Leigh's knees went rubbery with shock. *There it is,* she thought frantically, *the reason she made me promise in ignorance.* Gran had known Leigh would never knowingly agree to shoulder such a horrendous burden of responsibility. It was bad enough that anyone would let such a huge sum of money ride on a single poker hand, but to place the outcome in the unwilling hands of an innocent bystander . . . Leigh stared at Gran as if she could transmit her horrified thoughts by eye. But Gran returned Leigh's glare with a bland expression, a very small smile lifting the corners of her mouth, as if to say: *Too late now; you promised.*

Leigh saw the same bland look on Dow's face, but with the additional touch of malicious smugness. Was *he* the one who'd got her into this? Leigh wondered with a flare-up of her old suspicions.

As if Gran read her mind, that lady now said, "Since Leigh plays better poker than I, it was very generous of Dow to accept what amounts to a handicap when he agreed to let her take my place."

When Gran indicated that the two players should take their seats at the poker table, Leigh shuddered, closed her eyes in a brief but fervent prayer, and gave herself up to the mercy of Fate. Dow unfolded his long body from the embrace of the soft sofa and took his place at the table across from Leigh.

At a nod from Gran, Burt Cosgreve stepped to the table and began to shuffle the cards. While he did so, Gran said, "You're both experienced enough poker players to know that the luck of the cards is the least of this game. I know you'll each make the most intelligent decisions you're capable of. Play your best with the cards you're dealt . . . and win or lose, I, for one, will be satisfied."

Holding the shuffled deck in the palm of his hand, Burt offered it first to Dow and then to Leigh. Each drew out a card and flipped it up on the table, Dow the ten of clubs and Leigh the five of spades. Burt announced, "Dow draws high card. Dow deals and calls the game."

Leigh, grateful for any lessening of the heavy responsibility she felt, was relieved that this most important decision was Dow's. She looked up at him, waiting to hear his choice of game, and shivered to see the blank look of nonrecognition he returned.

He said, "I'll name the game . . . five-card draw. But I'll refuse the deal." Then in a flat, emotionless tone, Dow added, looking directly at Leigh, "You've impugned my integrity for the last time, Miss Mallory. *I* trust *you* to deal honestly, even supposing you were sophisticated enough to deal from the bottom of the deck, but I know you won't grant me the same trust. So, you deal, and then there can be no trouble arising from that area."

Leigh's face flamed as if she'd been slapped. But because she felt she'd earned his dislike, and richly deserved his scorn, she made no reply, only stared miserably down at the deck of cards in the middle of the table.

Then, in a more mellow, almost kind tone, Dow said, "Come on, Leigh, let's get this over with; deal the hand."

She snatched up the deck then and deftly dealt out five cards, face down, alternately to Dow and herself. She laid the remainder of the deck to one side, and as one, Leigh and Dow picked up their cards and with impassive faces each surveyed the hand.

Leigh held five cards of middle rank: one club, one diamond, and three hearts. The chances were only fair that she'd draw another heart and nearly nil that she'd draw two more hearts for a flush—a powerful combination of five cards of the same suit. Her best hope to win the game was to pair up either of the two highest cards in her hand.

Five-card draw was a game only a little less austere and stringent than five-card stud. In neither of these games was it common to win with overblown and opulent combinations like full houses, flushes, and straights. A pair of humble fives or eights could win in five-card draw.

Observing the etiquette of the game, Leigh unobtrusively cupped her hand and waited quietly for Dow to come to a decision and indicate that he was ready for the draw to be dealt. At any other time,

Leigh wouldn't have believed her talkative, lively family of kith and kin could be so still and quiet. But she noticed nothing of her surroundings now and only vaguely heard an occasional ping of a sherry glass and the low hiss and chuckle of the fire at the end of the room. Instead, her whole being was centered on this bizarre situation into which she found herself manipulated.

From beneath lowered lashes Leigh stole a look at Dow's grave and handsome face. Even as aloof and cool as it was, Leigh's heart ached to know that whether she won this game or lost it, this might be the last time in her life she'd see that face. Certainly she'd never again see it soften with passion or light up with laughter.

But as awful as this ordeal was for Leigh, she realized that for Dow the outcome was potentially far more damaging. If he lost this game, he'd have to pay an enormous debt that he hadn't even personally incurred. It might deal his business a blow from which it would take years to recover. And Leigh knew now, without a single doubt, that Dow would pay if he lost. He would've paid even without this farcical poker game, the purpose of which Leigh still didn't understand. Perhaps she'd always known he was an honorable man, no matter how hard she'd tried to deny it.

It was her pride, her damnable, precious pride that had made her doubt him, made her say such terrible things to him that he'd never forgive her. What kind of woman was she, Leigh asked herself in shame, that made her think herself so special that one silly disappointment as an adolescent gave her the right to turn her back on the only thing in the world worth having? Because of a stupid and obstinate refusal—a cowardly refusal—to live with a heart open to life and love, she'd lost the chance to be loved by Dow Madigan. And deserved to lose it.

Despairingly Leigh thought that if there was any way she could undo the damage she'd done, remove the insult, erase the accusations, she'd do it gladly. Not to make him think well of her again—if indeed he ever had; she knew that wasn't possible. Every expression in his eyes, every movement of his body told her Dow despised her and always would. But if only she could know—even much too late—that she'd behaved honorably too, so she could face herself in the mirror without disgust. But Leigh thought sadly of the ruefully true little poem by Emily Dickinson: "A word is dead when it is said, some say. I say it just begins to live that day." But Leigh knew those words she'd said to Dow Madigan would live between them, malignant and unforgivable, forever.

Into the waiting hush of the room Dow suddenly spoke, startling everyone. "Three cards," he requested curtly, throwing down the three discards from his hand. Leigh, dealing him three new cards from the deck, assumed he was drawing either to a pair already in his hand, or going for three of a kind, or keeping two high cards hoping to pair one of them, as she herself hoped to do.

When they each picked up the new cards and studied them, the waiting hush grew even more intense as the others in the room awaited the imminent outcome of this poker game that would surely go down as legend in the annals of Carmel-by-the-Sea.

Leigh stared down at the horrifying sight in her clenched fingers. Her heart jumped in her breast, her mind moved into high gear in a desperate search for a way out of this agonizing dilemma which had been thrust on her so unfairly. Almost in panic she looked up at Dow, but saw nothing in his face to help her. He met her glance briefly, his expression a perfect example of a "poker face," then lowered his eyes once again to his hand.

And then, like an answer from the spheres, Leigh's mind played over Gran's recent words, and suddenly, in a flash like spring lightning, with stunning and liberating clarity, Leigh knew what to do.

Shortly, Dow asked, "Ready?" Leigh nodded stiffly. Dow displayed his hand on the table: a pair of aces with a jack kicker and two miscellaneous cards.

Every head in the room swerved toward Leigh. She shut her eyes briefly, shuddered and folded her cards face down on the table. "I can't beat a pair. You win, Mr. Madigan."

A little storm of gasps, whispers, and groans filled the tense air of the room. But even now, when he was freed from the staggering debt of a quarter of a million dollars, Dow's face showed no sign of emotion. He rose stiffly from his chair and walked toward Gran. She looked very like a monarch in her dark blue dressing gown, her fine-boned face crowned by a halo of white hair, sitting upright and regal in the chair by the fire.

Dow lifted Gran's hand to his lips and kissed it,

bowing slightly. "Are we quite quit on this matter, dear lady?"

"Yes, my dear boy, we are," Gran replied formally. "Give me your note and a pen."

Dow handed her a piece of paper faded with age and limp from a thousand refoldings. Gran spread it open on her lap, smoothing it with a carefully tender hand, her dark almond eyes shining with tears. "Get me something to write on," she said brusquely, and John Channing made haste to hand her a copy of *Pacific Horticulture* lying on a nearby table. Placing the aged note on the magazine, Gran scrawled in her dramatic hand, "Paid in Full," dated it, signed it, "Jane Campbell, aka Persia Parnell," and handed it back to Dow.

Then she said, "I hope you'll humor a sentimental old woman, Dow, and allow me to keep my copy of the note as a remembrance of your grandfather."

Were those tears Leigh saw gleaming in Dow's eyes as he nodded and turned away, putting the canceled note into the pocket of his shirt? Or was it only Leigh's own tears through which she looked at him so longingly?

Dow cleared his throat and in a muffled voice said, "I'll leave you all now. I hope everyone will believe me when I say that in spite of the sometimes harrowing moments we've had together"—here he broke off to laugh in a painful, ragged way—"I wouldn't have missed it for anything. It would've been worth a quarter of a million and more just to meet . . . all of you."

Moments later John walked Dow to the door, and he left Illyria without a backward glance. In the sitting room all was quiet, the air thick with depression and defeat. Leigh, for one, knew if she tried to speak she'd begin to weep. Finally, with an impatient sniff, Gran rose from her chair and walked to the poker table. With one quick, deft movement she flipped Leigh's discarded hand face up.

John crept near, as cautious as a tightrope walker, and soon he was followed by Dibbie, Annie, and finally Burt. John, as usual, was the first to find his voice. In a high-pitched, bewildered tone he said, "But, look here, Jane . . . Leigh threw in a heart flush!" He looked up from the hand with shocked dismay. "Leigh cost you half a million dollars, Jane—she lost the game on purpose!"

Gran patted John's shoulder and smiled a secret message to Leigh. "She may have thrown in the winning hand, John, but Leigh didn't lose the game."

By ten o'clock that evening the house was settled down and quiet. Knowing sleep wouldn't come all night, Leigh lay on her bed still fully dressed. When she heard a light tap on her door, she expected Dibbie to come in. But it was Gran, carrying an object in her hands Leigh couldn't make out in the gloom of the dimly lit room.

Gran made her way across the room, and when she reached the edge of the bed, Leigh saw that she carried the antique Russian tea canister she kept on the dressing table in her room. Many's the time Leigh and Dibbie'd heard the romantic tale of the White Russian prince who'd escaped the revolution with his life, three diamonds, and a few objets d'art, one of which was the canister he'd given to Gran in the twenties as a memento of their brief but warm friendship.

"Why aren't you asleep?" Leigh asked softly.

"I'd ask you the same, but I know the answer. You're wondering if you did the right thing, aren't you?" Gran said, smoothing Leigh's tangled hair from her brow.

Leigh sighed and shook her head confusedly. "No, I think I did the right thing, Gran. I know I did what you *wanted* me to do. But I still don't understand . . . why did we have to play that game at all? I know *I* doubted him"—Leigh flinched from the memory—"but *you* knew he'd pay. And now, if he ever finds out what I did . . ." Leigh began to weep from fatigue and emotional stress. "I want to know why we played that idiot game!" she demanded.

"That's why I'm here," Gran said briskly. She took the lid from the canister and emptied the contents onto Leigh's bed. Out tumbled souvenirs and trinkets: single earrings whose twins were lost; rosebuds faded to a wistful pink; calling cards in elegant, spidery scripts—all mementos of a long, dramatic, and eventful life. Among the charming litter was a packet of envelopes and papers tied with a faded lavender satin ribbon. Gran handed these to Leigh. "Go on, open them," she said as Leigh looked at her hesitantly.

When released from the ribbon, they whispered dryly as they tumbled out onto the pastel coverlet of Leigh's bed. Poking gingerly through them with a gentle fingertip, Leigh studied them curiously.

"Here. This is the one," Gran said, plucking one out from the group and handing it to Leigh. "The others are all the same—more or less."

The paper she held was Gran's copy of the note, which Leigh hadn't seen up close earlier that evening. Scrutinizing it, Leigh saw that it had every legal requirement of a valid note: the amount of debt, the date, the place signed, and the signatures of the parties involved. That it carried neither an interest rate nor a due date was unusual, but not unheard-of, and certainly not illegal. But what riveted Leigh's attention and her dawning understanding was the garish thousand-dollar play-money bill affixed by a ruby-headed hat pin to the bottom-right-hand corner of the note. Under the faded signature of a once-young but now-dead Dow Madigan, Leigh read the dashed-off message: "To my angel, Persia—payment on account. Unlucky at cards, but so lucky in love—and never a loser so long as I have you. With love, your Dow, forever."

Leigh's eyes filled at the message so sweet that its power remained to move the heart after fifty years. In a choked voice she whispered, "It was only a joke, then. All of them"—she shuffled gently through the pile of papers on her bed— "just souvenirs, keepsakes from old friends and lovers. . . ."

"That's about it," Gran said gently. "I never dreamed that he would keep it too—or that it would be found and . . . misunderstood."

"But, Gran, why didn't you tell Dow? Why did you put him through that humiliating charade of the poker game when you knew he owed you nothing!"

Jane Campbell showed a rare sign of uncertainty and even guilt in the indignant way she answered her granddaughter's question. "Well, it was certainly as much *your* fault and *his* fault as it was mine!" After a pause she went on vaguely, "Things just got out of hand. . . . I told you the truth when I said I'd forgotten about that note, Leigh. At first, anyway. If Dow had brought it up promptly, I would have told him. But by the time it was out in the open and all that fuss and turmoil between the two of you started . . . well, I just thought I might be able to use the note to . . . well, fix things up."

"Fix things up," Leigh said flatly. "How so, pray tell?"

"Now, Leigh, you know if I'd told him the note was a joke *after* you'd accused him of intending to welsh on it, he might not even have *believed* me. He might've thought I was making some sentimental sacrifice to let him off the hook you'd hung him on. That would've *mortally* offended him. So I thought if I sort of . . . well, compromised between telling him and not telling him, by making him the sporting proposition to resolve the debt on a hand of poker, it would solve everything!"

Annoyed at the still-skeptical look on Leigh's face, Gran cried, "Don't you see? If he'd won the hand, *really* won it, I mean, then he'd have saved both his honor and his face. Just exactly as he's done now. And if he'd lost; if you hadn't thrown the game— and, Leigh, I was *sure* you would—well, I'd have just had to confess. That part *was* a gamble, I admit, even though I did my best to encourage you to throw the game by telling you the money would be yours, so you wouldn't feel any guilt about losing for *my* sake. It's true, though, if you hadn't done what you did, it would've been a very nasty scene when Dow found out what we'd done. . . ."

"*We'd* done?" Leigh said.

"All right, *I'd* done. But now you see how well it's all turned out."

Leigh laughed hopelessly. "Gran, he hates me. He'll never forgive me for the terrible things I accused him of, and I don't blame him." Leigh sighed heavily in resignation.

In a timid, sorry voice Gran said, "Maybe he will, Leigh. When he's had time to think about it."

Leigh shook her head. "Gran, I truly hope this will be a lesson to you about meddling in people's lives," she scolded gently. "The only thing that's turned out well is that he doesn't know how thoroughly he was had. If you think he'd have been mortally offended before, imagine how humiliated he'd feel now! He'd be livid, Gran."

With a worried look on her tired old face, Gran said conspiratorially, "Let's make a pact, Leigh. If you'll promise never to tell anyone what we've . . . *I've* done, I'll give you my solemn word that never again will I meddle in anyone's life. Not even yours, dear child."

Chapter Twelve

A few days before Christmas, Leigh and Dibbie accepted a "Last Chance for Lunch" invitation from Minnie Wanamaker before she turned her house over to Elaine and Dow and removed herself and her spirit friends to that mecca of the bizarre, Los Angeles.

She'd dressed up for the occasion in a lavender velour pantsuit that made an interesting contrast to her hennaed hair. To mark the holiday season, she wore on her bosom a little red-and-white Santa Claus face corsage made of felt and white puffed cotton. Minnie pressed second helpings of crab salad on her four young guests, but only Pamela succumbed, taking another honey bun as well.

When Leigh had first learned that Elaine Stanley would attend the gathering, she'd feared it would be awkward to socialize with Dow's sister. But it wasn't. Aside from possessing that rare social gift of seeming to belong wherever she found herself, it seemed to Leigh that Elaine went out of her way to be congenial to Leigh in particular. She admired Leigh's new blue wool dress, asked her advice on hairdressers and dentists and other matters she could just as well have discussed with Pamela. It was obvious that the two were already fast friends.

During lunch, Pamela again prompted Elaine to tell Minnie her reasons for moving to California. When the rueful tale of Dow's lady friend running off with Elaine's husband was finished, Minnie surprised them all by not finding it amusing, but not finding it tragic, either.

Nodding matter-of-factly, she commented, "The girl did the right thing. Obviously she divined that your brother's heart was holding back, waiting for another." Then, after looking into the middle distance for a short pause, she added, "Of course, your husband and the girl don't love each other either. But they'll serve each other well enough, temporarily, as companions in their search for the Significant Other."

When Minnie left the table to bring the dessert from the kitchen, the four young women looked at each other silently, with various expressions of skepticism, amusement, and thoughtfulness. Leigh said musingly, "The thing is, I've never known her to be wrong about anything."

When Minnie returned with a golden, crusty pecan pie smothered in whipped cream and set it down in the middle of the polished pine country kitchen table, she added as if she'd never left the room, "That lady friend of your brother's has great emotional intelligence, you see, Elaine. Some women are just naturally smart about knowing who truly loves them. Others have to be hit over the head with a two-by-four before they get the message."

Minnie bent over the gorgeous pie, and Leigh glanced around the table at the others. But the amused smile faded from her face as she saw that instead of watching Minnie cut the first piece of pie, they were all looking straight at her.

Christmas was bittersweet at Illyria. Leigh and Dibbie's mother and stepfather called from Gstaad to extend season's greetings and to say they were cutting their holiday short because of an administrative emergency that had come up at the base, which would prevent them from coming home for Twelfth Night. Leigh was touched to see how the others doubled their efforts to make the season merry enough to make up for the sisters' obvious disappointment.

The traditions were all observed. The greenery festooning the house smelled as pungent as ever. The brandy punch on Christmas Eve was as potent as always. The neighborhood children caroled as sweetly as ever on Christmas night, their fresh, young faces gleaming in the misty winter air. From her commission on the Wanamaker sale, Dibbie'd bought Leigh two season tickets to the San Francisco Opera, so she could take a guest. But in spite of all this, the lackluster quality of the season made everyone at Illyria hope that the coming new year would soon heal Leigh's heartache.

The one entirely happy event of the season was the reunion of Sam and Marianne Nelson. Sam called Leigh to tell her the joyful news shortly before Christmas, but it wasn't until Leigh ran into Marianne in the post office a week after the holiday that she had a chance to hear all the details.

After gathering their mail, the two young women walked down the sidewalk, still crowded with bustling after-Christmas shoppers and exchangers.

"Oh, Leigh, I can't tell you how wonderful it is to be back home where I belong. Christmas this year was everything it was ever meant to be," Marianne said with quiet joy.

As Leigh listened to her happy voice and noted the glow in her contented eyes, her own heart's soreness eased somewhat. How good it was to know that somewhere, someone had the good sense to rescue a valuable relationship from the cheap and transitory lures of these faddish times. When they reached Leigh's office, she asked Marianne if she'd like to come in for a cup of coffee.

"Thank you, Leigh, but I can't. Sam and I are going to Tahoe for the weekend, and I have to pack." Then she added with a sweetly wicked smile, "It'll be just the two of us."

Laughing for the first time in weeks, Leigh asked, "Will you be home in time for Twelfth Night?"

"Are you kidding? Would any loyal Carmelite miss Twelfth Night?" With a jaunty wave good-bye, Marianne called as she walked briskly away, "I'll bring you a snowball from Tahoe!"

Leigh went into her office, sat down at her desk, and studied the empty space on the wall display board where the picture of Minnie's house had once been. What a lot had happened since that day Dow Madigan walked in here looking for a house; and how badly it all turned out, except for Minnie Wanamaker.

Leigh remembered Minnie's remark at lunch about the Significant Other. Yes, that described very well what the still-healthy and sane part of Leigh's heart had recognized in Dow the moment he'd walked into her life. But she'd allowed that other part to guide her, that warped, cowardly part of herself still resentful over a past hurt that now seemed a mere surface scratch compared to the mortal wound she'd since suffered. If she'd had any spirit or courage, any *emotional intelligence,* she'd have known that anything as precious and rare as love was worth taking some risks for.

The jangling of the phone at her elbow startled Leigh from her mournful thoughts. It was the manager of the local bank where Leigh kept her personal accounts. He sounded both worried and excited as he told her, "Leigh, the most incredible thing just happened. A quarter of a million dollars was just deposited in your account. Do you know anything about it?"

Leigh groaned inwardly. "Yes, I'm afraid I do."

"Oh. You do know about it. Well, I just thought you might not . . . I mean, it was deposited into that small household account you hold jointly with Jane. That's a *checking* account, Leigh," he said with the horror only a banker could feel at the thought of so much money standing idle even for a day in a non-interest-bearing account. "It was a cashier's check drawn on a New York City bank and signed by the comptroller of a company called Madigan and Stanley."

"Does my grandmother know about it?" Leigh asked.

"Yes, I called her first because the check was made out to her." He paused, then said carefully, "I think perhaps she'd rather have told you herself, Leigh . . . that is, she didn't exactly tell me not to tell you . . . but one could've got that impression. But, I thought . . . well, I just thought you ought to know immediately. I hope I haven't started any trouble?"

Leigh laughed ironically. "No, you did the right thing, believe me."

When Leigh thanked the manager and hung up the phone, one thought as glaring and relentless as a neon sign flashed into Leigh's mind. In order for the money to be returned, Dow would have to be told the truth. She shuddered to imagine what the consequences would be when he knew. Well, she thought resignedly, it couldn't really be any worse than it was now. It might as well end in a bang as the whimper that now prevailed.

"He must be told," Leigh said firmly.

With a sulky frown, Gran protested, "But, Leigh, you promised."

The two women sat at the kitchen table late that afternoon in the quiet, empty house. Leigh felt giddy at the role reversal between her usually directive and bossy grandmother and her own conciliatory self.

"All right, then," Leigh said with ill-concealed

impatience, "you tell me how we can return that money without eventually having to explain why."

Gran shrugged. For an hour now they'd been over and over that problem, and no solution had yet come to light. The truth will out, Leigh thought sardonically. And there was a scrupulous part of her that felt Dow *should* know the truth, even though she dreaded his wrath as much as Gran did.

Finally Gran sighed mightily and shook her head. "I can't think of anything right now, but I will. Just let me mull it over for a bit," she said thoughtfully.

Leigh looked at Gran suspiciously. She knew she shouldn't leave it up in the air like this, but she was so sick of it! And, too, given Gran's marvelously devious mind, she actually might think of something. "Well, all right," Leigh grudgingly agreed. "But I'm only giving you a week, Gran. If you haven't told him by then, I'm going to."

"Don't threaten me!" Gran snapped with guilty defensiveness.

"I'm not threatening you, and you know it. I'm just *warning* you," Leigh said, surprised at how quickly she'd got used to her new role.

Many years ago, the parishioners of All Saints' Episcopal Church initiated the celebration of the ancient medieval custom of Twelfth Night on the Carmel beach, and gradually the village as a whole joined in. So it was that twelve days after Christmas, on January 6, the residents of Illyria set out at dusk for the beach at the foot of Thirteenth Street. Those Carmelites who lived too far to walk came in cars, their dismantled Christmas trees lashed to the roof or protruding from open trunks. Others walked, like Leigh and her family, dragging their trees behind them, meeting up with neighbors along the way, exchanging season's greetings. Everyone was in a holiday mood, looking forward to the exciting conflagration to come, and later, to the bone-warming soup supper served afterward back at the church.

The older contingent of the family wore wool slacks for warmth and sneakers for the sand. Leigh and Dibbie wore jeans and boots. Leaving her hair down for warmth around her neck, Leigh gave little thought to the rest of her clothing and was content to throw on an old black turtleneck sweater under her everyday trench coat. Fashion was not the order of the day at Twelfth Night.

When Leigh and the others reached the site, the great mountain of trees was already many feet high. Dressed warmly against the chill drizzle in the darkening air, people milled about, clustered in groups, laughing and chatting. Children ran about in delirious happiness while an occasional dog played hide and seek with the mercurial frothy waves at the edge of the beach.

It was nearly dark when the carols began. Leigh shivered with many unnamable emotions as she heard the several voices of her loved ones surrounding her: Dibbie and Annie's clear, sweet sopranos; Gran's slightly quavery but still-strong alto; John's reedy tenor; and Burt's sturdy baritone—and off to the side, the rich, full voice of a stranger, as deep as the tones of an organ—all raised together in singing the carols of old. When the last refrain trembled and died on the moist night air, the priest began the prayer of thanks for the year now past and blessed the fresh new year just begun.

When the lovely solemnity was over, a stir of anticipation ran through the crowd as the brave man who would light the fire stepped toward the gigantic pile of trees. The signal was given, the torch was thrown, and with a thrillingly dangerous whooshing boom the dark night sky exploded into orange flame. A great communal sigh of awe rose from the crowd as they pressed back away from the searing heat, from the deafening roar and crackle of the fire hungrily consuming the dry and brittle pines.

Leigh stood mute, mesmerized by the sight, lifted out of herself by the sheer magnificence of the force that electrified the night. No wonder, then, that she jerked in fright as she suddenly felt herself loosely embraced from behind and heard the dear voice she'd thought never to hear again whisper into her ear, "Hello again, California."

Whirling around within his arms, Leigh looked up into Dow's face, burnished copper in the light from the bonfire. Her heart leaped with joy as she breathed the words, "What are you doing here?"

"I live here, remember?" he drawled, smiling into her eyes.

"Oh, yes, of course," she stammered, feeling a fool again before him.

"Still forgetful, I see. I guess nothing has changed." But wasn't there a hint of a question in his voice? Or was it only a fervent and desperate wish that made her think so?

Then Leigh remembered that something indeed had changed, and obviously Gran hadn't met her deadline. If she had, Dow wouldn't be standing here on the city beach with his arms around Leigh, smiling into her eyes. Come to that, why was he, in any case? Removing herself gently from the circle of his arms, where she had no right to be, Leigh drew a quavering breath and prepared to tell him all.

"One thing has changed," she began. "I know I was wrong to accuse you of trying to manipulate Gran."

Laughing comfortably, Dow put his arm around Leigh's shoulders and walked her a few feet away from her family. With rich affection in his voice, he gave her a quick hug and said, "Never mind that now. I know you had your reasons, as silly as some of them were. But the idea of manipulating your grandmother is about as likely as a summer breeze doing battle with a hurricane."

Dow took from his pocket an envelope which Leigh recognized as one of Gran's, and handed it to her. In the flickering shadows from the great fire, Leigh saw inside five playing cards, all hearts, a replica of the hand she'd thrown in that awful night of the poker game. She looked down at them while searching for something to say. Unable to think of anything better, she mumbled hopelessly, "She promised me she wouldn't meddle anymore."

Again Dow laughed. "Yes, so she told me when she called. But she claims the promise became null and void when she was forced to tell me the truth about the note.''

So he knew! Leigh thought fearfully. Then why was he reacting so mildly? To forestall the outburst of anger that might come at any moment, Leigh rushed into speech. "I can't tell you how glad I am you finally know the truth. It's been horrible. I assure you, if I'd known the truth about the note, I'd never have let her put you through that charade. . . ." And then a disquieting thought stole into Leigh's mind. "Dow, you won that poker game not knowing the note was a joke. Why did you deposit the money in Gran's account after you won?"

As if it were the most natural thing in the world, Dow casually reached out and pulled Leigh into his arms again and held her closely as he explained, "The real question is: how did I ever let her inveigle me into that blasted game in the first place? Even now I can't remember how she did it. Somehow, she made it seem a way to show you my intentions were honorable . . . Oh, I don't know. I was so desperate to prove myself to you that I couldn't think straight and I was afraid that nothing I could say would convince you, so I agreed to the game.

"But after I'd been away from her bedazzling influence for a day or two, it seemed to me that winning that poker game really didn't prove anything one way or the other. If I'd *lost*—and paid—that would've proved something." Dow paused here and grinned conspiratorially at Leigh. "But now I see that was never even a possibility. Anyway, I finally realized that the best way to prove to you I was sincere was to simply pay the damned debt. So I did."

Leigh was struck dumb with delighted wonder that Dow had been desperate to prove himself to her. Before she could respond, suddenly from behind her came the sound of a frantic crackling and a whoomping unheaval as the madly burning mound of trees shifted and resettled, sending a million sparks skyrocketing into the blackness. As the crowd oohed and aahed, Leigh heard John Channing's high voice call out, "Did you see that, Leigh?" Then, as she watched him look around for her and not find her, he again called, "Leigh? Where are you?"

As she started to answer, Dow put his finger against her lips and whispered, "No, wait. Watch."

Standing close together, giggling a little like naughty children, they watched Gran reach out and lightly punch John on the arm, point vaguely in the direction where they stood, then pull him by the sleeve of his coat so that his back was to them. Then they saw Gran peer into the dark, lift her arm in a brief wave, and turn her own back squarely on them, her face to the gloriously flaming spectacle.

In a voice so warmly intimate that it sent shivers down Leigh's spine, Dow said affectionately, "You see? Gran's keeping her promise not to meddle, after all."

Leigh burst into laughter, and together they laughed in a wonderful moment of shared enjoyment. When the laughter ran down into comfortable chuckles and sighs, Dow kissed her. He kissed Leigh in a way she'd never before been kissed. She felt such a flood of love for him that her whole body felt full of warm and sunny liquid gold. As she returned the tender pressure of his lips, she vowed that never again would she ask for more than this moment, for this alone was reward enough for all the pain she'd suffered because of him in the past.

When he lifted his mouth from hers, Leigh clung to him still. "I'm so sorry," she whispered into his chest. "I've been such a disgusting fool. You have every reason to hate me, to never forgive me for all those terrible things I said to you."

Dow took Leigh's chin in his hand and lifted her head to look into her eyes. "Hate you? In all my life I've never met a woman who would have thrown away a quarter of a million dollars for my sake. The kind of women I've known have sold me down the river for an expensive bauble from another man, or left me in the lurch for a trip to Hollywood. But *you*—I know love can't be bought, but if it could, my darling Leigh, you paid a noble price with priceless gifts—selflessness, loyalty, faith, and love."

"Dow," Leigh said shakily, "I can't let you think I deserve all those wonderful things you've said, because I don't . . . I really don't. What I 'threw away' was never really mine. It wasn't even real."

"Yes, it *was* real," Dow said firmly, "because you *thought* it was real." He cradled Leigh's head in his hands then and kissed her mouth with great tenderness. "I tried very hard to resist you, you know," he said, his mouth moving from her lips to her eyes to her brow, where he buried his face in her mussed and tawny hair. "But I never had a chance. From that very first day, I knew I loved you, even while I taunted and insulted you in a hopeless attempt to resist you."

"Oh, Dow, I felt the same, but I never guessed. On Thanksgiving, you were so angry . . . I thought. . . ."

Dow quickly bent to brush Leigh's lips with his and stop her words. "I know, my darling, I behaved like such an ass that day. Because I'd been so rotten to you the day before, I assumed you were paying me back." He laughed shortly. "It seemed an awfully clever and efficient way to make sure I'd never be accepted by your family, if I'd walked into your home and not recognized the famous Persia Parnell—as well as the very woman I owed so much money to."

Shyly Leigh asked, "And do you understand now how I could've forgotten to tell you who Gran was?"

Dow pulled her closer to his chest and murmured into her hair, "Yes, my darling, I do see, now that I know you felt the same that first day. If love drove good sense from my head, it could certainly have driven mere details of family identity from yours."

Warm tears of relief, and gratitude toward life itself, moistened Leigh's closed eyes. The future that just hours ago seemed utterly bleak was now full of promise. He'd forgiven her, he even said he loved her. Surely from a base so strong as that, even Leigh, an "emotionally unintelligent" woman, could hope to build something of value.

"Do you remember that day on the tower?" Dow

whispered in Leigh's ear, causing her body to shudder at the memory. He'd said that day, " 'Some lucky day each November . . .' "

Leigh nodded, unspeaking, as his mouth again covered hers possessively. When the kiss was ended, Dow held her close, as if to press her into his body forever. From over his shoulder Leigh saw the glory of the fire, at its zenith now. It flared so brightly that the sky above was light as day, and she knew that meant it soon would die.

"Look, Dow," she said quietly, "look at the fire."

He turned, and after a moment's pause he said, "It looks as if the beach is on fire. Now that it's ordained by Fate, you have no choice but to marry me."

Leigh smiled at him uncertainly. Was he joking? A fresh start, she could believe in; even eventual success. But a proposal of marriage—now? Could it really be true?

"I know you said that . . . that you wouldn't marry until the beach went up in flames, but you were only . . . Oh, Dow," she said yearningly, "do you really mean it?"

He gave her a little shake. "Of course I mean it. I've always meant it, my darling reluctant lover. Do you need to be hit over the head with a two-by-four?"

Leigh laughed low in her throat and smiled a secret smile. Sighing, she replied, "Yes, I guess I do, at that."

Then for the first time Leigh reached out to Dow as if she had a right to, and took his fine, strong face between her gentle hands. She kissed him firmly on the lips, then said, " 'Some lucky day each December great waves awake and are drawn like smoking mountains bright from the west and come and cover the cliffs . . .' "

And the kiss that Dow returned to seal tomorrow's promise and all tomorrows to come was a kiss as pure and rugged and eternal as the clean white beach on which they stood, together at last.

Silhouette Romance

15-Day Free Trial Offer
6 Silhouette Romances

6 Silhouette Romances, free for 15 days! We'll send you 6 new Silhouette Romances to keep for 15 days, absolutely free! If you decide not to keep them, send them back to us. We'll pay the return postage. You pay nothing.

Free Home Delivery. But if you enjoy them as much as we think you will, keep them by paying us the retail price of just $1.50 each. We'll pay all shipping and handling charges. You'll then automatically become a member of the Silhouette Book Club, and will receive 6 more new Silhouette Romances every month and a bill for $9.00. That's the same price you'd pay in the store, but you get the convenience of home delivery.

Read every book we publish. The Silhouette Book Club is the way to make sure you'll be able to receive every new romance we publish.

Silhouette Romance

ROMANCE THE WAY
IT USED TO BE...
AND COULD BE AGAIN

Contemporary romances for today's women.

Each month, six very special love stories will be yours

from SILHOUETTE.

Look for them wherever books are sold

or order now from the coupon below.

$1.50 each

Silhouette Romance

___#49 DANCER IN THE SHADOWS Wisdom
___#50 DUSKY ROSE Scott
___#51 BRIDE OF THE SUN Hunter
___#52 MAN WITHOUT A HEART Hampson
___#53 CHANCE TOMORROW Browning
___#54 LOUISIANA LADY Beckman
___#55 WINTER'S HEART Ladame
___#56 RISING STAR Trent
___#57 TO TRUST TOMORROW John
___#58 LONG WINTER'S NIGHT Stanford
___#59 KISSED BY MOONLIGHT Vernon
___#60 GREEN PARADISE Hill
___#61 WHISPER MY NAME Michaels
___#62 STAND-IN BRIDE Halston
___#63 SNOWFLAKES IN THE SUN Brent
___#64 SHADOW OF APOLLO Hampson
___#65 A TOUCH OF MAGIC Hunter

___#66 PROMISES FROM THE PAST Vitek
___#67 ISLAND CONQUEST Hastings
___#68 THE MARRIAGE BARGAIN Scott
___#69 WEST OF THE MOON St. George
___#70 MADE FOR EACH OTHER Afton Bonds
___#71 A SECOND CHANCE ON LOVE Ripy
___#72 ANGRY LOVER Beckman
___#73 WREN OF PARADISE Browning
___#74 WINTER DREAMS Trent
___#75 DIVIDE THE WIND Carroll
___#76 BURNING MEMORIES Hardy
___#77 SECRET MARRIAGE Cork
___#78 DOUBLE OR NOTHING Oliver
___#79 TO START AGAIN Halldorson
___#80 WONDER AND WILD DESIRE Stephens
___#81 IRISH THOROUGHBRED Roberts

- -

SILHOUETTE BOOKS, Department SB/1
1230 Avenue of the Americas
New York, NY 10020

Please send me the books I have checked above. I am enclosing
$_____ (please add 50¢ to cover postage and handling. NYS and
NYC residents please add appropriate sales tax). Send check or
money order—no cash or C.O.D.'s please. Allow six weeks for delivery.

NAME_____

ADDRESS_____

CITY_____ STATE/ZIP_____